Dedicated to my best friends, Helen and Michelle, who have already travelled half way through this crazy life with me.

<u>Why Dragonfly Skies?</u>

I love dragonflies. Not only are they one of the oldest insects in the world, but the humble dragonfly also exists in so many beautiful sizes and colours.

They are born in water, spending their entire youth as nymphs hidden away in the safety of their liquid surroundings until they are mature enough to emerge in their true form into the insect world. Taking the first breath of fresh air, they unfold their delicate, powerful wings, learning to fly and adapt to their unfamiliar surroundings. In that final form, they live their short lives to the fullest, filling the skies with a rainbow of colour before they eventually fade and die. Spiritually they symbolise transformation, freedom, growth, maturity and adaptability.

They are symbolic of all mature women who carry with them the wisdom of youth and can adapt to their ever-changing bodies, using the strength they have gained from their unique life experiences to display their true inner beauty in their later years. Just like a dragonfly, as we get older, women will go to any length to avoid unwelcome sexual advances from the opposite sex.

Chapter 1

Have you ever just felt like stuffing a bag with all of your essentials, booking the cheapest flight to a hot destination, then after sticking your middle finger up at your life, running away from everything and everyone you know? After a day from hell and an evening practically begging my best friends, Sam and Julie, to join me, that is precisely what I did.

Let me introduce myself. I am Lizzie, a recently divorced, menopausal, middle-aged woman in my late forties. I have cellulite, more wobbles than Rowntrees and my breasts have now become more acquainted with my waistline instead of sitting quite pert on my chest where they had spent most of their life. I am sprouting hairs in places where they shouldn't be found on a woman. My body has recently created its own tropical climate, which could be the main reason behind global warming. In actual fact, I am pretty sure the environmental activist, Greta Thunberg, has recently started stalking me on Instagram for this very reason. I could have been used as an alternative heat source for the entire planet if they found a way of plugging me into the grid. Even my nipples are exhausted from the rapid temperature changes my body is inflicting upon them.

My weight is another issue. I hate everything about myself. I am too short, too fat and too saggy. I find myself judging my appearance against the many women of my age that I see in my weekly magazines so much that I comfort eat. I have an endless need for wine, coffee, carbs and chocolate, which isn't helping at all. No matter how many times I moved the scales across the bathroom, hoping to find that one spot on the lino that made me a few pounds lighter than the other ten places I had already tried, I could not hide from the fact that I was getting fat.

In the past year alone, my diets have taken me on quite a journey. I have been a vegan activist and sucked my way through an entire week of nut-milk and veggie smoothies. This resulted in me almost camping out in the bathroom, as the toilet became my best friend. I had a short-lived stint as a caveman on the Paleo diet, which didn't last too long as I could not live without my Friday night pizza. I even fasted like a Muslim through Ramadan, which made me uncontrollably pass out without warning, not great when you live alone. No matter what fad diet I tried the scales just kept climbing uncontrollably like the current bitcoin trend.

Even if I lost a few pounds, none of them gave me any lasting results. In fact, after I had succumbed to my normal eating habits, they had possibly made the weight gain worse. I was sure I was allergic to healthy food. It either gave me either diarrhoea to the point I could not leave the house or constipation, which bloated me and added a few more unwanted pounds to the scales. That's why I gave up trying to lose weight in the end. It was my excuse for my seemingly uncontrollable weight gain. It had absolutely nothing to do with the liquid lunches that I would often slosh down my throat during a coffee afternoon with one of my best friends, Julie. In fact those afternoons never actually included any coffee at all unless it came in the form of a Tia Maria cocktail. But those afternoons were the one of the many reasons I got through the menopausal years with my sanity intact.

Mind you, if I had possibly stopped drinking and shaved off my unsightly bodily hair, then I am sure I would instantly have been half a stone lighter. Right now, I could potentially braid my underarm hair, join a peace core and chant my way skinny. The only time I can say I frantically shaved almost bald was for my smear test, and that was only once every three years. This was out of sympathy for the young nurse who braved the sight of so many aging vaginas on a daily basis. At least they could then actually locate my elusive labia with ease and without combing apart my unruly pubic hairs that hid the entrance to my abandoned love cavern like a cascade of jungle vines.

So it all really began after my divorce. I had lost my way a little and completely stopped caring about myself. Although, when I actually consider things, I think I stopped caring about myself way before my husband left me. Throughout my married life, I had always willingly accepted the demands of my role as a loving wife and doting mother, losing the real me in the whole process. I forgot about my own needs. I had often sat in the silence of my home, staring into space, wishing my life away over a cold cup of Tetley and dreaming of what I could have been. Why do we do that?

Why do we just forget our own dreams and then allow ourselves to fade away into old age? I have no excuses now. I can do as I please yet I still feel so guilty putting myself first. Even though I was glad my marriage was over, part of me always felt something was missing. I no longer had a purpose.

Our marriage had not been great for many years, but like many things in my life, I just got on with it and swept the obvious under the rug that we were given thirty years earlier as a wedding present. This is where I swept everything that needed to be dealt with at a later date. Just like my dreams, everything seemed to be fading into the abyss of time, along with my own mortality.

I had always wanted to travel the world. After finishing the sixth form, I had intended on packing a rucksack and heading out into the great unknown for a gap year of adventure before returning to study for a law degree. I had wanted to see so many different countries and experience so many cultures before finally settling down. Then, at that fateful Friday night disco at our local rugby club, just before I sat my A level's, my direction in life changed. Dave walked into my life, and everything I had planned was forgotten. We were young, naive and full of romantic dreams for our future. I lost my virginity to him on the back seat of his rusty VW campervan and quickly became pregnant. That not only stopped all my gap year plans but also decimated my career in law.

We got married quickly before my pregnancy became too obvious, and I became the talk of the town. We moved into a small two-up, two-down terraced house in the suburbs just on London's outskirts. It was not perfect, but it was adequate. I gave birth to Tom and almost immediately became pregnant with our second child, Emma. At the tender age of 20, I already had two children under two and no career. Once I became a mother of two growing toddlers, I finally understood that Star Wars' scene where Yoda gets so tired of answering Luke Skywalker's questions that he just closes his eyes and died. I was mentally and physically exhausted at all times.

But, I persevered through those sleepless nights, endless days of teething, the toddler tantrums and the dreaded potty training. I felt a failure as a parent as they reached the Kevin and Perry teenage years. I didn't really consider how well Cathy Burke and Harry Enfield portrayed this moment in a child's life until I was living it. My son actually regressed into a past life mimicking that of a primitive life form. He only left the darkness of his bedroom in search of any unhealthy snack he could gorge on from the seemingly endless supply of food that he needed to consume. He grunted his way through almost every conversation I attempted to have, had lost all ability to string more than two words together to form a sentence and didn't speak properly for at least three years until he had reached twenty.

And then there was that fragile eggshell atmosphere of having another menstruating woman in the house. Some weeks it was a loving mother-daughter relationship, and others, like walking into a cat brawl as our PMT cycles clashed. And the horrendous father daughter arguments as she attempted to leave the house plastered in makeup, wearing the smallest piece of clothing covering only the bare essentials and looking like one of the Pink Ladies from Grease. Why did they become so argumentative and aggressive as they got older? Had I raised them wrong and not been such a great parent? Yet, in all the madness, I still kept it together.

One night as we sat eating fish and chips during a re-run of Blankety Blank on the TV, I told Dave the plans I had given up for him and how I still wanted to travel the world someday. So, with Les Dawson chattering away in the background, we made our own dreams. When the children had eventually left home, we would sell everything, buy a campervan and visit all the places that we had spoken about over the years. That was enough to keep me going through the worst moments of parenthood. It gave me something to look forward to.

But it didn't happen like that. We became submersed in our family life, Dave was the bread-winner and I was the doting housewife. I rushed around like a blue arsed fly trying to get the kids to their different after-school clubs on the opposite sides of the city, as Dave worked long hours just to bring in enough money to cover the bills. As time went on, we just seemed to lose sight of each other. The dreams we had once shared had been long forgotten. Everything became routine, including our marriage, and the feelings of Groundhog Day manifested into my everyday life.

I no longer needed a shopping list when visiting the supermarket as it was the same meal, the same night every week. There was no spontaneity or experimenting with new dishes. It was always the same routine. Mash and pie Monday, chicken curry Tuesday, pork chop Wednesday, pizza Thursday, fish shop Friday, spag bol Saturday and roast day Sunday. And just like the menu, there was no excitement in the bedroom either. In the early days of our marriage, as soon as the kids were having tea with their friends, we would rush upstairs for a quickie, just like we had been during our teenage years. It kept our relationship alive for a while.

Eventually, as the children grew older and spent more and more time out with their mates, boredom stepped into every element of my life. I managed to get a part-time job just to get out and meet people. I loved socialising and chatting, but Dave was not really that bothered. As I would talk away about anything that popped to my head just for conversation, he would stare blankly at the kitchen wall, nodding his head occasionally as he chewed on his pork chop. It was almost as if he had a filter in his mind that he used to capture just enough information to know when to acknowledge me. I knew he really wasn't interested in anything I said.

After dinner, all Dave wanted to do was drink beer, stuff his face with chocolate and watch his favourite TV programmes. I could hear his annoyingly loud laugh through the floorboards as I soaked away the night in a hot bubble bath. Everything he did seemed to irritate me. Even the sound of his breathing and eating brought me close to murder a few times. After putting my hair in curlers and spending at least an hour smearing my entire body with Nivea, I would place socks on my hands and feet to trap in the moisture and climb into bed alone, looking like an oversized baby. If he had wanted an affair at that point in our marriage, I wouldn't have blamed him. I was enough to scare away any man.

I guess the end of our marriage had really started a little over three years earlier when I hit an all-time low. My two beautiful children had flown the nest to embark on their own adventures, leaving my life very empty. I had spent years looking forward to having my life back, but when it finally happened I had no clue what my purpose on this Earth actually was any longer. I had most definitely lost interest in my general appearance, putting on over four stone since having my children. The weight had crept on gradually, so I hadn't really noticed how big I was getting until I needed a size 18 in clothes. Then it affected me physically and mentally. I had no self-esteem and would hide away in oversized clothes. Dave hadn't seen me naked in years. This affected our relationship deeply.

By the time the children had left, it was almost as if I had hit an oil patch at just forty five years old and I was now skidding uncontrollably through my middle ages towards my own lonely grave. Dave and I were like complete strangers. We hardly spoke, hardly went out together and slept with our backs to each other. We hadn't been physical in years. After a heart-to-heart one evening, we decided to make a bit of effort for the sake of the investment that we had made into marriage.

Instead of spending our weekends sat on opposite sides of the settee watching re-runs in silence, we decided to spend time doing things together. We visited stately homes, historical gardens and different UK cities. We had a weekly date night's and got dressed up to go to posh restaurants. But even as we ate oysters surrounded by oppulence, we sat there in complete silence. We no longer had anything to say to each other. But at least it was a distraction to what was really going on. Our marriage was dying, and so was my mind

Chapter 2

Then I found out he had been cheating on me with a gym bunny over half his age. They met at a private health club that we had joined together to help with our failing relationship. I was hoping it would speed up my metabolism, address my weight issue and add some spice to our non-existent sex life. It definitely injected some spice to his life. Still, for me, the only spice I got was from the five-piece girl band that blurted their "girl power" anthem through my headphones as I struggled for breath while attempting to climb the equivalent of the Eiffel Tower on the step machine.

Sweating my way through another gruelling session like a red-faced hippo, I ignored the inner me that was begging to give up and head downstairs for a mid-morning latte with a fresh cream slice. Instead, I kept my eye on the prize, that slinky red dress with matching coloured sex kitten heels displayed in the shop window at M&S. I could wear it to the Christmas meal with my best friends and wow them with my new toned curves. All I wanted was to be able to strip naked without scaring myself in the bedroom mirror as my unfamiliar overweight reflection wobbled past to take a shower.

As I tried unsuccessfully to reduce the belly apron that now replaced where my vagina used to be, the gym bunny squatted her perfectly toned Lycra-clad glutes, almost on the face of my testosterone pumped, bench pressing, cheat of a husband. Twerking her way through an all-over body toning routine, her perfectly applied makeup did not even smudge one line of sweat down her flawless, youthful skin. Her hair remained neatly tied in a top bun as she jogged effortlessly next to me. The only wobble that everyone could not miss was from her very obvious surgery-enhanced double "D" sized breasts that bounced hypnotically, to the delight of all the males in the gymnasium.

To cut a painful story short, I eventually relinquished my quest for bodily perfection and gave in to my morning craving for cream slices. On the other hand, he became a gym junkie and started to train daily, seven days a week. He also took up an evening class straight from work a few nights a week. He became a health freak, a vegetarian and only ate low-fat meals, rejecting the comfort food we had survived on for years. I could no longer do the regular shop without remembering his protein powders, protein snacks and soy-based alternatives. He became obsessed with his daily workouts, counting his calories and reducing his fat intake. It was like being married to Mr. Motivator without the spandex. I would have commended him if it hadn't have been for the affair. At least one of us was making an effort on ourselves.

He began to take an interest in his appearance for the first time in years and wearing clothes that would have better suited a teenager. He casually mentioned maybe going to a music festival with his friends to tick something off his bucket list. He didn't have any friends or even like music. He constantly moaned about turning the "racket" off the radio as I bopped along like a teenager to Wham as I boiled some eggs. He point-blank refused to watch "Strictly Come Dancing" with me on a Saturday night. So I used to take a packet of Hob Nobs to bed and watch it on my own. I had always loved dancing. Dave had once too. We used to dance together in the kitchen to the old romantic songs that played on Steve Wrights Sunday love songs. The radio had always been my companion. It helped me get through the monotony of the day like an old friend chattering away in the corner. It was better than the silence that had moved in after the children had left.

Dave also had his ears pierced and came home with his first tattoo after years of telling me how horrendously chav they made people look. Our bathroom shelf became more stocked with male grooming products than Boots, as manscaping became his weekly religion. He had less hair on his body than me, which wasn't that hard considering I had given up entirely on making my vulva neatly trimmed for any unexpected visits. There had been no regular watering of my bush in many years.

When he began wearing aftershave to his evening fitness classes, I became very suspicious. I became a private investigator, trying to catch him out with random questions. I noted how often he picked up his phone. Sniffed his clothes for any clues to his infidelity and observed his body language to see if he was lying his way through our failing marriage. I became an international code breaker, trying unsuccessfully to find out his passwords to access his online social media accounts to see if he was messaging anyone I didn't know. I fast became obsessed with proving his unfaithfulness just to punch my case-solving triumph into the air.

How did l catch him out? I rang him one night to find out what time to expect him home for dinner. Instead of declining my call, which l presumed he had meant to do, he answered. l endured a fully explicit three-minute call, listening to his animal grunts as he banged away, like a rampant rabbit, while his accomplice let out an occasional porn star-style moan. After her pleads for him to rub her clitoris, they both reached a perfectly timed climax together. That's when I knew she was faking it. I had never had an orgasm the entire time we had been married. He had no clue even where to even find my clitoris. As we had sat watching yet another repeat of Top Gear, I had once casually thrown the question "So what's a clitoris, Dave?" into the advert break, just before popping to the kitchen to make a cup of tea.

"Everyman knows what one of them are! It's the newest Hyundai import isn't it? Them Japanese come up with some great names for their cars! Clit-oris…makes it sound really futuristic, doesn't it?"

I almost gave myself away on the phone with a loud chuckle with thoughts of him telling her that instead of him giving it a rub, he would take it to the local car wash to give it a good jet wash after he had finished. I was pretty impressed with his stamina, considering he had told me the reason for our non-existent sex-life was that he suffered from impotence, and he hadn't wanted me to feel bad about not being able to make him erect. That was why I had become firmly attached to B.O.B., my battery-operated boyfriend. He knew exactly where to find my clitoris.

After hanging up, I had no clue how I was going to deal with the situation. I should have packed his bags and kicked him out. Or I should have left a note on the kitchen table and disappeared into the sunset. But I chose to play along to see if he came clean. In a kind of sick and twisted way, it became quite enjoyable. Knowing he was lying as he made up a pretty creative story about how hard his session at the gym had been that night was hard not to react to but I kept the act going for sometime. As he settled down to do some accounts, I caught him punching in his password on his laptop one evening as I placed a cup of tea on his desk and planted a false tender, loving kiss on his disgust balding head. This gave meal the access I needed to find out exactly what he was up too while he was busy "at the gym." From then on, the revenge game stepped up a level.

I felt sick as I read their messages back and forth, but it allowed me to really mess with his head. She had sent him a link to a figure-hugging dress that she had planned to buy for a sordid weekend away that he had booked. I bought myself the exact same dress but in a much bigger size. I squeezed my voluptuous curves into my spandex and I served up his evening meal, almost passing out from the lack of oxygen that was reaching my lungs. His face was a little confused at first, but he just told me I looked nice and carried on eating his full-fat beef mince shepherds pie. Unknown to him, I fed him as many saturated fats as possible just to clog up his arteries in hope that he would pop his clogs. That would have made everything much easier.

After a night alone feeling sorry for myself, crying my sorrows into a bottle of vodka, I woke up with a killer hangover and need for a little vindictiveness. So I topped up his favourite bottle of aftershave with a squirt of the strongest, first stream of the morning, "Eau de urine." Splashing it on his face after getting himself ready for another gruelling evening gym session, I handed him his kit bag and smiled smugly to myself as he headed out through the door to meet his gym bunny covered in my stale piss. I know it was childish, but it gave me just a little bit of satisfaction.

Every Wednesday evening, he met up with his bit of fluff straight after work in M&S for a "Dine-In" meal for two in their restaurant accompanied by a bottle of Pinot Grigio. I would find the receipt in his coat pocket the following morning before he woke up. That evening, I would serve up the same food that he had eaten with her the night previous with the exact same bottle of wine. This went on for weeks. How he didn't twig that I knew baffled me.

After a while, I tired of the games. Looking at him actually made me feel physically sick, knowing that he could lie so openly, disrespecting the mother of his children without any remorse. After another restless night caused by night sweats and hours of dwelling on lost dreams, I casually asked him for a divorce as I placed his usual scrambled egg and bacon in front of him. He called me all the names I had expected. I was crazy and needed psychiatric help if I thought he would dare have an affair. I was totally out of order snooping through his personal messages. Of course, it was my fault, as I had let myself go and lost my sense of humour. If only he had known the extent of my pranks, I thought my sense of humour had been entirely on the ball. I had given him my best years, and he still couldn't give me the respect of being honest. He stuffed his gym bag with all his clothes and left, leaving me sitting at the kitchen table, sipping my morning coffee as Fleetwood Mac "Go Your Own Way" blasted out on the radio.

Chapter 3

Those first few months of being alone were the hardest. I hated coming home to an empty house. At night I would shut the curtains and eat myself to the point of stupidity. My muffin tops had now transformed into a three-tier wedding cake, and I fitted into none of my clothes. Leggings and oversized t-shirts became my daily attire. At least they stretched with my ever-expanding waistline. It was when a pair of my favourite knickers no longer covered my pubic region that I realised just how much weight I had gained. No matter how many times I adjusted the silky material, part of my oversized mon-pubis spilled out from the gusset sides like a saggy old testicle. I despised what I had allowed myself to become. All I wanted to be able to see my vagina again when I looked downward. I hated myself.

That's when my daughter suggested that joining an online dating site would boost my self-esteem. That was an experience in itself. We started by setting up a profile on a dating site designed for the more mature client. We struggled through at least twenty different poses for the perfect profile picture that would either mean instant rejection or gain a second glance from someone who quite possibly had failing eyesight. A photograph is fine for the youngsters that bloomed in any light. They have no deep wrinkles to capture the shade and create contours that shouted out your real age through a megaphone no matter how much you tried to appear younger. Even applying makeup that was supposed to make you look instantly more youthful and flawless just made me look like a tired, old transvestite.

Then as she wrote my bio, which made me feel as exciting a catch as a Dover sole. Dull, flat and blended in with its surroundings.

"Attractive mature woman in her late forties seeks a thoughtful romantic to join her for adventures, long walks in the country, nights at the pub and dancing. The things I am most passionate about are helping others and making people smile. My friends describe me as warm, generous, thoughtful and caring."

Go to the pub and go out dancing? I can go to the pub and dance all night with my friends. I don't need a man to do that with. Go for a walk? I already walked far enough after Dave took the family car filled with his belongings to his bimbo's flat. Plus, the thought of my overweight body squeezed into a set of waterproofs was not the most appealing vision for a blind date.

My whole profile was really based on the hope that a passport photo and twenty quid a month would bring love or at least a nice meal out and some sweaty sex with a stranger. Yet as I swiped through most of the choices of balding middle-aged men that stood in their puffed out and sucked in Action man poses, all I could think was, "Would I like them bearing down on me?" Most decent-looking men of my age didn't want an overweight middle-aged woman suffering from vaginal dryness to take to the pub with them. They were all on a younger dating site, lying about their age and living their mid-life crisis years to the fullest. Why did mine have to be so...sensible?

I wasn't after a cardigan wearing pensioner who wanted a replacement for his late or ex-wife to cook him his usual ham, eggs and chips. I wanted passion, romance and excitement. Someone who made me laugh out loud and wanted to stay up past 10pm. Someone who would whisk me away for surprise European city breaks and danced away until sunrise. I wanted the kind of man I could get drunk on a bottle of whiskey, go skinny-dipping and make love on the sand with as the waves caressed our naked bodies. Someone a bit like Billy Connelly with bigger biceps. Instead of standing up for my inner voice that was screaming its frustration inside my dying brain, I just went along with her idea of my perfect man. After all, everyone else always seemed to think they knew what was best for me.

Then the dates began. There was the one who spent all night talking about himself and didn't bother to ask a single question about me. Another who immediately sent me a dick pic and asked me, by text, if he should reserve a room in a local B&B ready for after our first date. The one that arrived in a Northface jacket expecting a female version of Scott of the Antarctic, who on spotting me swigging my pint of lager and stuffing my face with smoky bacon crisps, swiftly turned on the spot and didn't even stay for a drink. Then the classic ten-year out-of-date photo guy who I walked straight past as he was no longer sporting a full head of hair, neither did he have gleaming white teeth. In fact, I don't think his teeth were actually his own. After giving it just one month, I concluded that it was better to just stay at home, do my nails, sew a quilt or clean the house to kill time rather than waste my life on a bunch of worthless dates.

Fast forward a year of costly solicitors, countless self-help therapy sessions and a ferocious financial settlement resulting in the sale of our family home, I was left with abox full of hurtful memories, a much healthier bank account and the lowest of low self-esteem. I moved into the spare room at my daughter's house and pretty much rode that year out on a rollercoaster of emotions with more ups and downs than a pair of whore's knickers. It finally came to a head on the day I received my decree absolute. Sitting at the kitchen table, I stared at its finality, sobbing my failure at life into a stone-cold mug of instant coffee. I had hit my lowest point, and there nothing to look forward to. With no motivation to sort myself out, my prospects of reaching 50 as a sad fat spinster were looking more likely.

As if the day hadn't already gotten off to a bad start, as I took a pee, something unfamiliar caught my eye. There hidden in the middle of my unkempt ginger pubic triangle, was a single white hair! I was utterly distraught. This was a defining moment of my mortality. My youth was fading, and the panic gripped me. Choosing to let myself go full bush made it impossible to hide the fact that my Mary was starting to lose its pert and perky appearance. It was either let her grow old gracefully and wear a natural hue like some kind of hippy feminist act, as I had imagined Dame Helen Mirren or Meryl Streep's pubes to be. Or, I could bow down to the dominant culture's expectations, try to delay the inevitable, and buy a Betty Beauty auburn hair dye kit for down there! My inner feminist broke, and I bowed to the social pressure that came with being a female. My crotch was supposed to be a fountain of youth. I couldn't let her down!

Picking up the telephone, I poured my anguish into Sam's ears and was told to stop my self-pity party, grab an overnight bag, pick up some wine and bring snacks. I didn't need persuading. A night with my oldest friends was the perfect remedy to every life crisis. I hadn't laughed in such a long time and I needed them to inject some humour into my static life.

If it hadn't have been for my best friends whipping my enormous arse into gear that night, I would possibly have thrown myself off the nearest bridge into the path of the 5:25am London to Swansea train. I couldn't see a way out or the rut I had dug for myself. My mind was becoming a mess, and I could no longer concentrate on more than one thing at a time. Multitasking was no longer the ability to do loads of things at the same time. It was doing something else while I tried to remember what I was doing in the first place. I found myself forgetting words and staring blankly into space as if I had forgotten every noun in existence. It was almost as if they had been sucked entirely from my memory one night as I slept. I could tell you every adjective that described the item I needed, its colour, size, shape or texture, but could I hell remember what the object was actually fucking called. It became the most frustrating game of charades I had ever played, only it wasn't a game. It was my new reality.

My emotions were all over the place. One minute I was raging at everyone that crossed my path. The next, crying like a blubbering fool to the teenage shop assistant in Lidl, as she scanned my microwaveable meals for one and looked desperately for help from anyone that caught her scared gaze. I put it down to depression caused by the divorce, but my friends were sure that it was "the change."

So, after a night emptying a few bottles of wine and with much persuasion from Julie and Sam, I visited my doctor to see if they could give a reason behind my sudden changes. As I walked into the consultation room, a male doctor who looked almost the same age as my own son flashed me a smile and said, "How can I help you today?"

Feeling a little embarrassed, I began telling him my symptoms, hoping he would tell me it was stress-related or depression. He went on to tell me that my symptoms were similar to so many illnesses, including that of alcoholism. But he didn't think that was the cause of my situation, even though if he had taken my blood at that moment, I would possibly have more alcohol in my system than Bargain Booze. So I plucked up courage and said the dreaded words. "Do you think it could be menopause?"

A sudden rush of redness flooded his youthful cheeks, and a few beads of sweat appeared on his brow, almost as if he had been too scared to approach the subject himself. He pushed himself out from under his desk, rubbed his sweaty palms on his legs, looked at me sympathetically from under his slightly steamed glasses and gently approached the subject.

"I don't know! It could be! There are no tests that I can do to give a definitive answer, as it affects every woman so differently. There has not been much research into it. I can do a blood test to check that your thyroid is working as it should be, and if not, we can put you on HRT. That might help a little with the hot flushes and settle the hormones, but it won't help with the weight gain. That is a natural part of the process, unfortunately. All you can do is eat well and do regular exercise to lose any unwanted weight. For some, menopause lasts just a few months. For others, it can last up to ten years. I can't really tell you much more. I'm sorry!"

Ten years! Ten years of this! I went to him for help, not a life sentence! There was no way I was going on HRT either. HRT patches were a way of slapping some glands on me to stop me drying out like a prune. My mother had taken them through her menopause and it had done her no favours no favours at all. Even though they had stopped her hot flushes, she had turned into a middle-aged acne riddled teenager overnight.

This was like going through adolescence all over again but without all that life ahead of me. At least with puberty, I knew the very moment when it had begun. Finding that first curly pube was the proudest moment of my teenage life, apart from the arrival of the small bee stings on my small double A-sized chest. Then my periods had started, and I had surpassed childhood. I was now a fully-fledged woman.

No moment defines menopause. There is that time in your early forties when you spend a minute researching the symptoms to prepare for what lies ahead. Then, over the next few years, you spend time arguing out loud with yourself after yet again forgetting your debit card pin number and, to make matters worse, forgetting where you wrote it down just in case you forgot it again. Then there's the hot flushes which are so damn inconvenient and confusing. I remember the first time I thought I was having a hot flush, I had been at Sam's and had panicked at the sudden increase in body temperature.

"Quick!! Feel my skin, feel it! I am having my first hot flush I am sure of it!"

But then she had reminded me that I had just stood to close to the kettle steam. And when they did actually start, I always had an excuse for a hot flush. I had worn the wrong choice of clothing, it was the messed-up seasons due to climate change or it was my uncontrollable weight gain that had created its own tropical climate.

There had been days that I had stood for an hour in the cold aisles at the local supermarket, wafting the freezing cold air over my blood red face and pondering about my hormones.

"Am I on the change?.... Is this THE menopause?.... Maybe I am just coming down with something, or maybe it is menopause....No, it can't be. I am still too young and wearing denim....Could it be, though...Is it?... Maybe? FUUUCCCKKK!!!!"

When you actually come to terms with the fact that it might be menopause, there is the realisation that, unlike puberty, you have no clue what you are becoming. It was like puberties evil aunt. From the vast amount of weight I had already gained and all the new hairs sprouting in the many unwanted places, like my nipples and chin, I was convinced that I was becoming my father! I was too young to be feeling this old!

The visit to the doctors had made me feel even more shit about myself. I grabbed a slice of chocolate cake, poured a mug of coffee and flicked on the TV. Scanning through the numerous channels, I located a vintage episode of "Wish You Were Here....?" presented by a glamorous middle-aged Judith Chalmers who looked so relaxed as she strolled barefoot on a deserted Greek beach. The sound of the waves lapping at the shore was bliss. The cloudless deep blue skies and clear turquoise seas seemed so dreamy, and the charming blue-roofed houses of the Greek village seemed so serene as it sat sleepily next to the pure white of the soft sand. How I wished

I was there at that very moment. I would do anything to be relaxing on that beach, surrounded by silence, apart from the lulling sound of the waves that would hypnotise my mind and calm my raging hormones.

I was so sure that experiencing menopause there would make it a little more bearable. Still, as a single middle-aged woman, I didn't dare to go it alone to a resort that catered for couples seeking romance or families looking for adventure. I didn't want to be that woman who entered a restaurant alone to the sorrowful whispers of the other diners that reached her with the sea breeze as she ordered a meal for one. If only there had been somewhere that did holidays for single middle-aged women that made them feel relaxed and welcome. I would have packed my bags at that very moment and left without hesitation. I could hide away from life, sharing my experiences with other single women who would quite possibly understand what I was going through.

That's when the idea actually first came to my mind. Maybe I did need to change my life or a holiday to get away from everything. Perhaps I could persuade Sam and Julie to tag along with me for company. We had never actually holidayed anywhere together in the whole time we had been friends. A week in the sun with my best friends could be the perfect remedy to the current rut I was stuck in.

Filled with excitement, I telephoned Sam and Julie, arranging to meet up for coffee. This ended up with us drinking our way through the happy hour "Two for One" cocktail menu. After an hour of trying to convince them both to join me while sweating my way through yet another hot flush like Fred West watching Ground Force, I made a slightly tipsy decision.

I was going to run away from my dreary life, regardless, and take a risk.

Inside there was a deep yearning to be that crazy wild teenager again full of dreams. I was taking no more crap, as there wasn't much more of my life left to waste. Greece was the perfect place for me to enjoy my single life and newly found freedom. I would go alone even if they said no, and I didn't even need to just stay for a week. I could stay for as long as my money lasted. And then I could get a small job in a restaurant to support myself. If it all went tits up, I could just come back having at least tried.

"You can't just up and leave for Greece. You're a mother! You have responsibilities and a life here. You can't just leave. What would we do without you, Lizzie? You're the mum of the group. The one who keeps us grounded. We can't be Charlie's Angels without the three of us. It just wouldn't be the same!"

"My kids are both grown. They have their own lives and don't need me here anymore. I have plenty in the bank from the divorce. Enough to support me for a while! You both don't need me around. You are always so busy at work, Sam, and you are always somewhere else in the world Julie. But you could both come with me! Come on, Sam, you could do with a break. You never take any time out. What have you got to lose? You are single. You have no kids. You are your own boss and, if you feel the need, you can work from anywhere in the world with a good internet connection. Wouldn't you rather be sitting in the sun, sipping a cocktail surrounded by handsome Greek men and blue seas? And you, Julie, you have no work commitments, no money worries and no current husband to tie you down. Who knows, you could actually find hubby number 4 or 5. How many divorces are you on now? Anyway, at least both think about it. We could experience a real Greek way of life and stay in a quaint cottage close to the sea. We could hire a car and explore the island. Maybe we could try out a few new things. Drink copious amounts of wine, eat olives and dance the nights away. Then we could watch the sunrise over the horizon as we sip on a mojito. It would be a crazy adventure, wouldn't it?

"Crazy is the right answer! I am too old for all that last-minute, unplanned shit now! I am no longer a carefree hipster happy with making do with sleeping in a donkey shed! I need luxuries. I just can't do it, and neither can you!

"Well, darling, I am more than happy to join you! Where should I sign! Tell me the date, the time we fly, and I shall be there! I will upgrade us to the first class, of course. I could not stand to be crammed into those ghastly economy class seats with a Saga tourist smelling like a urinal next to me. It would be quite an adventure, do you not agree, Sammie dearest? I think a holiday together for the first time would be quite divine. Who knows, I might find my own Aristotle Onassis. Life has become quite droll over the past few years."

"I knew you would, Julie! So we are going whether you come or not, Sam! But as you say, it really wouldn't be the same without the three of us. I need to do something with what is left of my life while I can still walk without needing a hip replacement!"

It didn't really take for Sam to make up her mind. I knew that Julie would have convinced her that it was a great idea. Sam had always been pretty easy to convince after consuming large quantities of alcohol. The phone had blurted to life just after 7pm that same night.

"Okay. I am in. You can't be going it all alone at your age. Who knows what trouble you would both get yourselves into. Just promise me that we won't end up in some run-down shack in the middle of nowhere. Let's meet up tomorrow night so we can plan it properly over dinner. I can't believe that I am agreeing to this!"

Chapter 5

I had known Sam and Julie almost all my life. We had gone to nursery together, we went to the same primary and secondary school, joined the same clubs and hung out with the same gang of friends. We were completely inseparable throughout our adolescent lives. We had always called ourselves "Charlie's Angels" after the popular 1970's TV programme, as there were three of us. Julie had to be Farrah Fawcett's character, Jill, because she had blonde hair and beautiful. Sammie took the role of head-strong Kate Jackson's character, Sabrina, and I was the sensible Jaclyn Smith, aka Kelly. These are pretty much the character roles that ended up following us through our lives.

Throughout our teenage years, we wore the same clothes, had the same hairstyles, listened to the same music, shared our first cigarette together, and lost our virginity around the same time. Even our boyfriends were chosen based on their friendship group so we could all have a boyfriend from the same gang. When I met Dave, Sam had got together with his best friend, and Julie had a fling with his older brother. But as we grew, we all gradually followed our own paths in life. And the directions we had followed were all very, very different.

Sam was the only one of us that actually made it to university. She was the academic member of the group. A high flyer that now ran a successful recruitment business for professionals with degrees and doctorates. This saw her travel all over the world. She spoke three different languages, Spanish, German and Mandarin and was always on conference calls with the HR departments of well- known international companies trying to find placements for her high-profile clients.

She made a fortune from her business, but she had never given her personal life a glimmer of hope with all the time she had invested in its success. This had meant that there had never been a long-term boyfriend or husband in her life. In actual fact, I would have challenged her sexuality if I hadn't actually been there when she lost her virginity in the back of the same VW camper moments after I had lost mine to Dave. She had had a string of boyfriends through university, but she completely lost interest as her business started to succeed. She ploughed all her energy and waking second into her career.

I had found this a little sad, as I had always thought that Sam had the potential to be a great life partner. She was always there for me when things with Dave had been too much to cope with. She picked me up when I felt low with her home-baked cakes, dry wit and sarcasm. She was very blunt and straight to the point, so you always knew where you were with Sam. She didn't have time for beating around the bush. I guess that was all part of the success of her business career. There was never a hidden agenda. Everything was factual, honest and in your face. She scared me sometimes with her sharpness and honesty. Of course, her observations were always right. She could see things from a completely different angle or dimension. One where rose-tinted glasses did not exist at all and sugar coating was made from salt. I, on the other hand, was a hopeless romantic and believed deeply in happily ever afters.

Everything with Sam was first class, five star or Michelin star. Nothing on her body was cheap or from the sales. Her clothes all came from the current season rail in Selfridges, gem-studded jewellery from Tiffany's. Her hair was cut by the iconic hairdresser to the famous Larry King in South Kensington. She refused to go anywhere without looking as if she was about to walk onto a promotional shoot for the business magazine, Entrepreneur. She had the perfect toned body from years of eating well and working out with her personal fitness instructor, Charles. He was twenty years her junior, but I am sure that he also made sure that she was well lubricated in all areas, although she never let on. It had been years since I had seen her with a steady boyfriend, yet she always seemed to have a smile on her face.

She was now reaching her late forties with not a wrinkle in sight to give away her age. This must have been from having no children of her own that caused us all to age rapidly with little sleep, little time for skin routines, constant stress and high anxiety. She just a few nieces and nephews, plus she had been an unofficial aunt to my children. She was not great with children. It didn't come naturally to her as she had never experienced her own maternal desires. She just felt awkward in their company, as she had no clue how to speak to them. Engaging in toddler babble was not the same as a high-profile board meeting in three different languages, although it had sounded just the same to me.

Then there was Julie. Julie had never needed to work as she lived off the income from her divorce settlements from her many ex-husbands. She was currently on divorce number 4. She seemed to sniff out money like a well-trained bloodhound. It had started in secondary school tiny wasp waistline and incredibly good looks had bagged her Tarquin, the richest boy in the school.

By the age of 16 and to the horror of his parents, who disproved their relationship, they became engaged. Then at 17, as an act of rebellion, they both skipped school one afternoon and ran away to Gretna Green to get married with no prenuptial agreement in place. After just a year of married life, Julie was already a divorcee and single, inheriting hundreds of thousands of pounds in a very public and high-profile divorce settlement. Tarquin moved from the area after every element of their family lives leaked into all the local newspapers.

Her encounter with Tarquin enabled her to learn everything she needed to know about being a successful gold digger. She left school with no qualifications, yet she was possibly the smartest person I knew at manipulating men into her sticky web. She knew where the elite hung out, the right questions to ask, what charity events to support, what to wear to attract the suitable victim and even which vacation spots to choose depending on their bank balance. When she found her target, she would do extensive research acquiring everything she needed to know about their relationship status, net worth, interests, failures, and weaknesses. The arrival of the internet simplified everything. It became her best friend as it saved her endless hours at art galleries, polo matches and theatre galas, just to eavesdrop on conversations to get the ammunition she needed to reel the next victim in.

By the time she was 25 she was already on divorce number two and amassed another fortune, which she invested in cyber stocks and shares. There wasn't anywhere that Julie couldn't go or hadn't already been. She spent her life on a non-stop holiday, including cruises, private islands and exclusive villas that cost a year's salary just to stay for a night. She had many one-night stands and was a bit of a slut. But when she met a potential husband she acted quite differently. She would become elusive and play hard to get.

These victims showered her with gifts from diamonds to apartments in cities across the world, just to try an woo her. She never put out on a first date with her this kind of target. Sex was not the initial transaction. She made them work for that and gave them lots of hope that that would be the end prize, insisting they got to know her first like any respectable man would. That made her even more desirable as she kept herself just out of reach enough to evoke temptation. Manipulating them into marriage was her main aim. After presenting her with an engagement ring with a rock the size of a lychee, she would show her appreciation and succumb to sexual favours, no matter how old, fat or ugly they were.

Her next marriage was to a Texan oil tycoon 30 years her senior. She moved to the USA for a few years, and we hardly saw her. She would occasionally turn up in London and send a taxi for myself and Sam to meet her for an all-expenses paid lunch. She lived the high life that most young women dreamed of. This meant that she hadn't needed to work a day in her whole life. Although she argued that being a gold digger was a full-time occupation.

After just two years of marriage, her Texan tycoon husband number three suddenly died of a heart attack while on their private Caribbean island, and Julie returned to the UK a very wealthy widow. Julie inherited his entire estate. His children contested his will and managed to obtain over half of their late father's money back in an out-of-court settlement. Julie wasn't a heartless woman and did have some empathy. With millions in her bank account, she no longer needed a wealthy husband. But Julie found it impossible to be alone. She needed someone to chase after, as that's how she survived.

Julie didn't grieve for long before she was back out there looking for wealthy husband number four and eventually met him at a charity event for Oxfam. She actually fell in love with husband number 4 for all the right reasons, and they seemed perfectly matched. Everything was going smoothly, and she was almost talking about having his children until she found him screwing the cleaner over the grand piano in the ballroom of their lavish stately home. He was the one who had broken her heart. Since then, she has remained single.

Now in her late forties, she has a home in France, the Maldives and California. She is still childless, although she has many stepchildren and step-grandchildren that she never sees. Most of them hate her or are much older than her. Every part of her had been stretched, stuffed and tucked to perfection, just like a comfortable settee that you don't want to throw away. It was like having an eloquent version of Dolly Parton as one of my best friend's.

Yet she was always just plain old Julie to us, and she never acted any differently around us either. Her money had not changed our friendship. We had all chosen different paths in life but found solace in our childhood friendships that seemed to keep us all grounded. We were now also all single, middle-aged and menopausal. That was something we couldn't run away from, but we could make it as enjoyable as we could.

Chapter 6

It was pouring with rain as I headed out to meet Sam and Julie. With my M&S raincoat zipped up to my chin and the elasticated hood pulled tightly against my cheeks, I waited patiently for the bus to come. I had not bothered doing my hair as the damp would cause it to frizz anyway, and what was the point of putting on any make-up. It would have just ended up running down my face making me look even more like an aging transvestite and quite possibly scaring the life out of anyone who crossed my path. I would freshen myself up in the lift before I reached the restaurant.

After almost an hour of waiting and being drenched from head to toe by the passing cars, the bus eventually turned up. Taking a seat next to the heating vent that sent a warm breeze of air around the bus, I pulled down my hood and gave my hair a tussle with my fingertips to allow any dampness to dry in the humid ambience. Looking out through the rain-smeared windows, everything seemed so depressing. At that moment, I hated everything about my life. I hated where I lived. The weather, the greyness, the city, the noise but most of all, I hated how I looked. As I gazed at my reflection in the bus window, I saw a drab middle-aged woman staring back at me. I was the kind of woman that I had once vowed never to become as I had wondered around in my perfectly lean youth wearing a skirt so short that the world could have been my gynaecologist. I was now...frump girl.

The bus had taken almost an hour to reach my stop at London Bridge, giving the hem of my dress enough time to dry. The rain had now stopped, but the clouds were still so dark and heavy as I followed alongside the dirty brown waters of the River Thames.   Eventually reaching the Shard, the elevator door was already poised open as if ready for my arrival. Pressing for level 31, I searched my bag to find the small compact mirror that I knew existed somewhere in amongst all the other useless items that had been stored in its depths for decades. In fact, if I had searched hard enough, maybe I would find the tiny hole in the bottom where I was sure my marbles were slowly escaping from.

By the time the elevator had reached level 17, I had located the mirror and applied my makeup as best I could. I threw my head downwards and ruffled my hair to give it some volume. Then I took off my middle-aged raincoat and folded it over my arm, revealing a rather sexy black A-line dress that flowed over my unflattering spare tyre. It was precisely what Gok had suggested as a tip to hide that menopausal belly on This Morning with Phillip and Holly. As the doors sprung open at level 31, I stepped out like a contestant on Stars in their Eyes, almost expecting a round of applause for the incredible transformation I had achieved in just a few rushed minutes.

As I wandered into the elegant, modern and chic establishment, I immediately felt out of place. Why couldn't Julie just be happy meeting at a Pizza Hut instead of somewhere that would possibly zap my entire bank account in one meal? Locating Sam and Julie chattering away to each other amongst the other diners, a young waiter took my raincoat and motioned for me to join them. The room was light airy and seemed to float in the skies above the cityscape below. From almost every angle you looked, vast panes of glass gave full 360-degree panoramic views of London.

Our table looked out towards the infamous giant penis skyscraper, the Gherkin. It was quite an impressive view to take in for many reasons, although even the size of that could not reignite my failing libido. I could have possibly spent an hour trying to locate so many familiar landmarks on the skyline, but that was not what I had come for. The only landmarks that I was interested in were ruined temples of Greek Gods with statues of naked men with much smaller penises. This was the only moment that I had to convince Sam that she was making the right choice, and I wasn't going to waste another second while my memory was working with me for a change.

"Darling, you look ghastly! Have a seat and take the weight off your trotters! You must have got drenched in that awful downpour. Did you really come by bus in this? You should have taken a taxi and had him drop you at the door. If I had thought, I should have asked my driver to pick you up after he had dropped me in. Anyway, I shall get us a bottle of the best champagne they have for us all to share! My treat! You are still drinking aren't you sweetie?"

"Thanks, Julie! Of course I am still drinking"

"Good because I am not stopping drinking with you just to support you. The last time I did it was the worst few hours of my life Darling let me tell you!"

Julie calls everyone darling or sweetie.
"You are still coming, aren't you, Sam? Have you both been here long? Am I on catch up?" I said as I noticed two empty hi-ball glasses with gin stirrers in the centre of the table.

"You are always on catch up! Two glasses of anything alcoholic with bubbles in, and you're under the table or on it anyway! And yes, I am still coming. I can't believe that I have agreed to go. I will need to stock up on valium to cope with you both!"

"It will be a scream, Sam! I don't know what you are worried about! It's not like we are going to end up doing anything stupid or get arrested. We are respectable middle-aged women now and not crazy teenagers."

"Darling, with the number of drugs you need to take daily, you will rattle your way through passport control. After a full body search, you will quite possibly be spending a few years in Greece behind bars without having to spend a penny unless you sort out a licence for all your pharmaceuticals," Julie chuckled.

It was true. I take drugs. I mean a shit load of drugs for absolutely everything you could think of. Then I take more drugs to help with the side effects of the other medicines I am taking. I take so many drugs that I forget what each one is supposed to be doing. Anyway, they make me smile, so they are working in general, unless I forget to take the drugs or run out and then it's a living nightmare trying to remember what I was taking that particular drug for. That was another curse of menopause. Facts like that no longer stayed in my mind for longer than a few seconds, yet I could still recite both Sam and Julie's old landline numbers from when we were just kids. I hadn't rung those numbers in almost thirty-five years! What was all that about?

Roaming the world freely with a bag full of drugs was potentially an issue. In my naivety, I honestly believed I could just chuck my medication in a bag and set off into the sunset. Julie explained that unless I wanted to be banged up in some hellhole prison screaming my innocence at a stern-faced Greek guard who wore a creepy moustache like a certified evil mastermind, then I would need to get a drugs licence. Yes, that is absolutely a thing! So rather than risk spending a few years with Borat as a company, I needed to make my stash legal. I made a note in my diary to make a call to the doctor the following day.

We spent the remainder of the evening looking at different Greek islands. Eventually narrowing it down to the islands of Samos, Kefalonia and Mykonos. After several more G&T's, a few more lists of likes and dislikes, we had made a decision. We were heading to Kefalonia. Without any hesitation, the flights were booked, and we were heading out the following week. I left the restaurant into the darkness of the night, feeling a sense of excitement for the first time in years.

The following morning I applied for my first ever passport at the tender age of 48. While sitting in the photo booth waiting for the camera to flash, I stared at the reflection of the unrecognisable women looking back at me, and for the first time, I could see how unkind I had been to myself. I had possibly been quite delusional about my own aging appearance. Every time I met an old friend from school, I had convinced myself that they must have looked way older than I did. But the truth was they were probably thinking the same when they looked at me. I had been in denial of my age for a long time.

I always knew I would get old, but I hadn't quite expected it to happen as quickly as it had. I had been kidding myself for too long that the silver strands of glitter that protruded from my once fiery strawberry blonde hair had actually been natural highlights. They weren't. I was going grey and I needed to accept it. I could do with a makeover and a new haircut to suit my maturing appearance. The unexpected flash almost burnt my eyes. I pulled back the curtain without waiting for the photo strip and headed straight to the nearest hair salon, booking myself in for a complete makeover that very afternoon. I wanted to change everything. I no longer wanted to be frump girl.

It also gave me a week to rapidly sort myself out. If someone had murdered me at that moment, my chalk outline would have quite possibly been mistaken for Mr. Blobby. I hated the thought of exercise. It just wasn't something I did. I seriously needed to shift some of the excess weight that I had accumulated around my middle. If only hot flushes had burnt calories, I would easily have been a size 8 in no time.

The girls were pretty supportive and offered their own secrets to their perfect size 10 figures. Julie had text me to tell me that she had been in contact with her dealer and ordered me a batch of magic pills that melted her excess fat. The only downside was that I would possibly not sleep for a few days causing me to potentially look even more haggard than I did. While Sam offered me the contact details of her personal fitness trainer who was pretty domineering, unforgiving and had a bum so tight that he could bounce off the walls. But all I really needed was someone to follow me around and slap unhealthy food out of my hand. Who the hell wants to touch their own toes anyway?

Ignoring my cravings, I started online morning fitness classes, power-walked everywhere and created a healthy eating regime that I could actually stick to. I lived on a liquid diet of smoothies and soup for an entire week and bypassed the local bakery on my usual morning walk. I stopped all the late-night snacks and glasses of wine, drinking green tea and lemon water instead. I was determined to like what I saw in the mirror. It paid off. I lost almost a stone and felt so much better. From which part of my body I couldn't actually tell, but I liked what the scales read. So as a treat, I decided to go buy myself some new clothes.

Shopping was quite an eye-opener. It had been many years since I had last bought myself anything new to wear, apart from that one-off dress when I was playing mind games with Dave, and that didn't really count. I didn't know where I should be buying clothes at my age. I walked into my old favourite, Top Shop, and as I looked through the skimpy undies and swimwear, that annoying Thong Song flooded my mind. The only use I could ever see at my age for a pair of crotchless panties was for my uncontrollable bladder. It would make that emergency dash to the ladies much easier for sure.

What was it with clothes that hardly covered any part of the female anatomy! Didn't they realise that half the British population was morbidly obese, and real women were not built like an extra from Baywatch? It was no wonder young women felt so pressured by the fashion industry that it messed with their mental health. It had already affected mine at the very thought of squeezing myself into one of these cheese string contraptions.

A shop assistant must have noticed me ruffling through the clothing rail, trying to find something a little more appropriate for my shape. Assumingly, she asked me if I needed help finding a gift for my daughter. When I told her it was for me, I was told that they were not sure they did my size. Could she not tell that I had starved myself stupid, sweated for a week and worked hard to achieve my new size-14 booty? Her words had stabbed at my self-esteem and popped my newly found confidence bubble with her cat claws. I resorted to shopping in Evans and M&S and feeling comfortable amongst the senior conservative shoppers in their timeless capri pants, forgiving stretchy leggings and classic beige cardigans. The added bonus was there were hidden tummy control panels in almost everything I bought.

Chapter 7

Having already consumed a few glasses of wine and a Diazepam tablet to calm my nerves, I followed Sam and Julie out into the damp darkness of the early hours. Looking like a line of frantic ants hurrying to get out of the rain, we followed the orderly queue of eager passengers along the wet tarmac and towards the flight steps. This was the closest I had ever been to an aeroplane. It was much bigger than I had expected, not that I had really ever thought about how big they actually were up close. I had only ever seen them on the telly, which never gave you any real idea of size as everything was small. It was quite unnerving to think that I was about to be launched at high speed several thousand feet in the air in a tin tube with wings carrying so much weight, floating above the clouds with my life entirely in the hands of a pilot younger than my own son. How could he have possibly racked up enough air miles for me to know that I would be safely transported to the other side of the Mediterranean and be on a beach by midday? I wouldn't even get in a car with Tom, let alone trust him to fly an aircraft.

As we reached the aircraft door, Julie ushered me into the three reserved front row seats to her right. Grabbing my flight case, she told me to take the window seat while Sam pushed our baggage into the overhead compartment before joining me. Sam and Julie had flown several times, yet this was my virgin flight, and I was already feeling the nerves unsettle as I watched the rest of the passengers find their seats. When all the passengers were seated and belted, the aircraft began its slow taxi to the runway, and the flight attendants started their safety demonstrations. That's when my stomach actually started to twist in knots. Why did they have to tell me what to do if we crashed! Would we crash? Would I even remember what to do if we were hurtling towards the ground from 36,000 feet at 500 knots? We hadn't even left the tarmac, and I was already considering my death! I was finding myself praying for the first time in my entire life.

Sam passed me a pear drop to suck on as the aircraft came to a stop. Then from nowhere, the engines started to roar, and the plane began to speed along the runway so fast that my head was thrust back into the headrest as I heard myself say "Holy Fuck!" without it meaning to escape my lips. I am sure that my face must have looked at least ten years younger for a split second as the aircraft suddenly lifted into the skies, and the ground below started to sink into the distance. I am sure my face must have gone through a spectrum of different colours as my stomach finally settled back into its normal position, and I let out a loud sigh of relief.

"Are you alright, Lizzie darling? You look terrible. You look like you need another drink. I will order us another G&T when they come around with snacks! It's just a few hours, and we will be on the ground again."

Those few hours were the worst moments of my life. With every shudder and shake of the aircraft, I found myself grabbing Julie's arm in fear. How did anyone find this enjoyable? Julie had slept for almost the entire way, and Sam had been lost deep in a travel book. I just felt so on edge. I couldn't even bring myself to look out of the window at the open expanse of the ocean through the clouds below me. I think I added a least few more brow wrinkles and crow's feet onto my face just from squeezing my eyes shut so tight for the flight duration. How the hell anyone managed to become part of the mile-high club, I had no clue. I couldn't even move from my seat to take a pee, let alone anything else.

The landing was the worst thing I have ever experienced. Surely they should put all first-time flyers in one of those simulators so that I knew exactly what to expect. As the nose of the aircraft dipped towards the ground and suddenly tilted to the side, I found myself unconsciously signing a cross across my chest and frantically searching under my seat for my life vest as I was convinced that we were about to plummet into the seas below. As we finally hit solid ground, throwing me uncontrollably forward as the brakes engaged, I was ready for a few drinks and a lie down to get over the horrendous experience. The worst part was I had to do it all again in a week.

As Sam riffled through the overhead compartment for our flight bags, I could not wait to step out of the aircraft. The brightness of the morning that was now spilling onto one side of the air steward who was stood smiling and nodding her goodbyes to the other passengers. As we reached the doorway, a warm breeze greeted me and almost swallowed me in a moment of divine pleasure. The sun on my skin was stinging with the sudden temperature change, and the sky was the most incredible shade of endless blue. My senses were already overwhelmed, and I had not even set foot on the dusty ground below.

With a gentle nudge from behind, Julie encouraged me down the steps and onto the hot tarmac to join the rest of the excited passengers heading towards the terminal. I had no clue what I was supposed to be doing next. Taking Sam's lead, I queued up and waited patiently for a scary looking guard behind a glass screen to scan me up and down with his expressionless glare before nodding his approval and letting me through to collect my suitcase. It was not the most friendly of welcomes I had expected, but I would not judge all the locals based on my first encounter.

Sam and Julie sauntered ahead and stood waiting at the baggage collection as I rushed to the ladies. As I hadn't dared to leave my seat for the entire flight, I needed urgent relief. My bladder was now about as useful as a chocolate teapot. When I needed to go, I needed to go. If my body had been a car, I would have happily traded it in for a newer model. As I had hit my middle years, I had very little control of my bowels. Every time I coughed, sneezed or spluttered, I either leaked or backfired or sometimes both. I used to laugh at my own mother for crossing her legs when she had to sneeze or cough to save herself from an embarrassing accident. It wasn't so funny anymore.

After freshening myself up and changing my Tenna pad, I re-joined the girls who were both looking so glamorous in their designer clothes as they waited patiently for plain old me to join them. Julie would get cross when I put myself down. She would remind me how naturally funny I was, and that was so damn sexy. I didn't feel sexy. I just made people laugh, so they didn't laugh at me. In actual fact, I can't remember the last time that I actually laughed and felt happy. I was hoping that this holiday would change this.

"So what now? Do you have any idea how we are getting to the villa, I need to get into something a little more comfortable!" Sam always wore trouser suits, even when she wasn't working. It was almost as if she constantly needed to express her own independence and emancipation to the world. But there was something quite undeniably intoxicating about her style. Almost like a modern man who was not scared to portray his feminine side by wearing a kilt or mascara. It was unambiguous to everyone that she was sassy, confident and definitely wore the trousers in her own life. In fact, it had been a long time since I had seen her wear anything other than her suits or gym wear.

"I have booked us a private taxi. It should be waiting outside to take us. I can't ever remember saying it was a villa, Sam. The write-up said it was more of a simplistic traditional style accommodation with a pool and sea views."

"Private taxi is just my style, darling! I couldn't think of anything worse than sharing a packed bus with a load of other ghastly tourists. It is almost eleven, and I, for one, am ready for a liquid lunch! Let's get a hurry on, shall we?"

Julie's drinking habit could have challenged Joanna Lumley's character, Patsy Stone, in Absolutely Fabulous. In actual fact, she was a lot like Patsy in so many other ways too. She was tall, thin, blonde, beautiful and often pissed by midday. Her success in life had been solely dependent on the good nature of others who had fallen for her sob stories. She had little contact with her own mother, who herself was an alcoholic and had conceived loads of children by several different fathers, most had ended up in care. She had no clue to her own father's identity as her mother had no memory of who had been that weekend's ejaculation due to her inebriation. This could have been the reason why she had an uncountable number of failed relationships and one-night stands sprinkled across the world without counting her several divorces. She had experimented with almost every drug known to man. She had explored her sexuality, having had a month-long relationship with an Australian woman. Declared that she had joined in many high society orgies and wife swap events, plus claimed to have woken up underneath Rod Stewart at a wild party in the late '90s, although she couldn't actually remember what had happened. Her life was colourful, and she did not lack confidence. If she wanted it, she would have it no matter what the cost.

Following the signs to the exit, we wandered through the arrivals door into the front of the tiny airport. Here, we were greeted by a large crowd of drivers holding pieces of paper with the name of their expected passenger almost illegibly scribbled in biro. You could practically smell the overpowering scent of testosterone mixed with strong tobacco that wafted in the stale, humid air of the tiny airport. We wandered along the line of men searching for our names, almost like an episode of Blind Date, until we reached a very handsome young man in his mid to late twenties. Julie had already devoured him with one look as she caught a glimmer of his perfectly toned and very muscular biceps as he reached out to carry her case. Running her perfectly manicured fingers over his upper torso, she came out with the tackiest one-liner I had ever heard.

"Oh my! Aren't you just a delight after such a tiresome journey! If you were a Transformer, you would most definitely be Optimus fine!
With Julie linking her arm into this handsome stranger as she stroked away quite inappropriately at his biceps, giggling away flirtatiously at everything he said, we struggled behind with our own suitcases. It was almost as if

our existence had been completely forgotten. As we put our bags into the car boot, Julie was already giving out her mobile number. This was most definitely a sign of how things would pan out for the remainder of the week. I had to give it to her, though. Even though she oozed femininity from every pore of her exquisite body, she had the biggest set of balls of anyone that I knew.

Chapter 8

"I can't believe that you messed such a simple task up, Lizzie! What the hell are we supposed to do now!! Just look where we are. There is no civilisation for miles around us, and there is no chance of us getting a hotel room in the middle of the summer holidays! I can't believe that I trusted you to book something for us. I knew I should have done it myself, but no, you were adamant that you had everything under control!"

"Look, Sam, I am sorry, okay! I had no clue that I had booked for Sparti in Greece! I thought it said Spartia. It's an easy mistake to make, isn't it! We should be able to find somewhere else to stay, I am sure!"

"Easy mistake if they were in the same country, but we are on an island in the middle of the Ionian Sea almost three hundred kilometres away from our actual villa for the week! How could you get that mixed up! Didn't you even think that this looked a little different from the pictures you saw online? I need a stiff drink to work out what we will do, as unless you have any bright ideas, Jules! Jules! Christ, where has she got too!"

I had messed up big time. How hadn't I noticed the mistake before now? I was so sure that I had booked everything correctly. I had even emailed the owner of the villa to confirm our time of arrival. What were the odds of two Greek villages of similar name in two completely different parts of Greece and both having a villa of the same name in their town? You couldn't have made it up. I had found it quite comical actually, but Sam hadn't quite seen it that way when we had come face to face with a young Greek couple in the throes of passion in the swimming pool we had thought was ours for the week.

After Julie had politely asked the confused couple to leave, the husband started shouting profanities at her in Greek and waved his arms about in objection to our unwelcome presence. Sam, not knowing what he was saying, suddenly squatted down and began to wave her rigid hands about in front of her like a ninja on the attack and began to chase the man around the pool. It was just like watching a scene from Carry On Abroad. As the confrontation became a little more heated, I took a seat on my suitcase and took out my phone. I recorded the whole thing for evidence of cause, and not so I could upload the video to "You've been Framed" for a chance of winning £200.

Things finally calmed down when the woman disappeared inside the villa and threatened to call the police. It was only then that Julie took my booking form from between my fingers and noted the error. After spending a few embarrassing moments apologising for Sam's behaviour and our intrusion, we wandered out onto the dusty narrow roadside, dragging our suitcases and found our way to the nearest bar.

As Sam disappeared to find Julie, I took another sip of the icy Cosmopolitan drink through the straw and looked out over the infinity of the clear turquoise Ionian waters. The calmness of the scenery seemed to soak into my veins and I really didn't care that we had nowhere to stay. I would have been happy to just sit in this exact spot watching the horizon for the rest of the week. It was so hypnotic and soothing as the gentle waves lapped at the pure white pebbles on the beach below. After just a short while Julie and Sam returned to the table with some news.

"It's all sorted sweetie. I have just been chatting with the most wonderfully charming gentleman at the bar, Milos. His son owns the tavern you know! Anyway, he has somewhere we can stay. He said it's a pretty basic but has everything that we need. It is just a few miles walk up the hill but his son is going to give us a lift in the back of his truck as it's quite a steep walk. So drink up sweetie, we can get ourselves settled and freshen up a bit before we head back for some food."

Knocking back the remains of my cocktail, I reluctantly pushed myself up from the chair and, dragging my suitcase, I followed behind like an obedient puppy. As we reached the front of the taverna, a Greek man in his mid-fifties, waited patiently to give us a helping hand onto the flatbed.

"Yasou! My name is Elias. I hear that you beautiful ladies have had a bit of bad luck since arriving in Spartia, No? No matter, it is all part of your adventure. I will take you to Papa's old house where you can stay. It is a steep bumpy drive so please hold tight. The house has been empty for many years, but it has comfortable beds and a shower for you all to freshen up! You will like it, I'm sure. Let me help you into the truck," he said with a friendly wide smile.

He was rugged and handsome in a way that I had expected of a Mediterranean man. His olive coloured skin was still youthful and framed by a thick head of course dark wavy hair that was pulled back off his face into a small ponytail at the base of his head. His large deep brown eyes seemed to seduce you quite willing without any effort. His perfectly straight nose led downwards his plump thick kissable lips. I felt the adrenalin surge through my body as the blood rushed to my cheeks making my face blush uncontrolably. Areas of my body that I had totally forgotten existed were also being stimulated by my thoughts. How could a simple look make me, a middle aged woman, react in this way. Other than that, I was having the most intense hot flush at the most embarrassing moment.

"I can manage myself thank you!" Sam said in her usual independent way and took it upon herself to ignore the extended hand of the handsome stranger. Effortlessly lifting her leg upwards, she pretty much stepped up onto the rear without a single struggle, then, settled herself on the floor against the cab. I sometimes wished that she wasn't always the feminist and would just let a man take the lead once in a while. I was pretty sure she would actually enjoy it.

Julie, being Julie, never turned down the chance to be in the arms of a complete stranger, allowing Elias to slip his hands around her tiny waist and lift her with ease in his strong arms onto the rear of the truck. She threw him a flirtatious smile as she playfully unwrapped her legs from around his waist. Teasingly, pushing him away with her hands as she elegantly swivelled herself onto her knees and thrust her backside into his face as she dusted down an area on the floor in front of her and smugly took a seat.

"I help you?" he asked as he noted my height. I must have been at least a foot shorter than both Sam and Julie. I could not have jumped up onto the back of the truck even if I was twenty years younger.

"Yes please. I am not as light as her though," I warned, as he gripped at my uncomfortably wide waistline.

"You are a beautiful woman with curves in all the right places for a real man!" he announced with a smile and lifted me with ease onto the rear of the truck.

I felt myself blush at his directness as he loaded on the suitcases, before locking the tailgate and making his way to the drivers seat.

He hadn't been wrong. The drive was extremely bumpy and incredibly dusty. He navigated the narrow windy steep streets above the taverna before taking a hidden track off the main road. The intensity of the suns rays against the hot metal had made it impossible to hold onto the side of the truck without burning my hands. I gave up trying to keep myself still and found myself bouncing around the back of the truck like a noisy fart in a cave. By the time we reached the house, I was laying vertically on the floor, crushed up against the tailgate with my dress up around my waist exposing my spandex. I was just glad that the bolts held up against my weight. The last thing I needed after the morning from hell was to find myself rolling off the side of a cliff to my death.

Elias appeared from the drivers cab and flashed a big smile as I quickly tried to retain some decency.

"I hope the journey was not too uncomfortable for you ladies."

"Nothing quite like having your entire body slammed violently against something hard!" Julie answered as crudely as always.

Elias smiled at her fleeting remark as he reached his hand inside the flatbed and saved me from flapping about like a seal as I tried to lift myself unsuccessfully from the floor.

"Please, I will bring your cases. If you could follow me," and with that he disappeared through a gate that led underneath a dense archway of greenery.

"That journey was ghastly, I can't believe I actually travelled in the back of a truck. I have snapped at least three nails on that journey! I will have to find a salon to get my nails done. I cannot possibly spend an entire week with them looking like this. If this place is terrible we shall be finding a five star hotel anywhere for the remainder of the week. I will pay for it myself. I need to get out of these filthy clothes, they are ruined!" Julie said looking down at a black oil stain that had covered the one side of her designer slacks.

We followed Elias through the gated archway and along a cobbled pathway that led through a tunnel of vines, hung with an abundance of ripe green grape bunches. Reaching upwards I picked a bunch and popped a small grape into my mouth. Its freshness burst on my palate and left a sweet after taste. As we reached the end of the tunnel, a pretty garden opened out in front of us filled with figs, olives and large pink Bougainvillea flowers. It was almost as if I had wondered into the Garden of Eden. A large table sat over looking the sea under the shade of a pagoda that supported the heavy foliage of an old twisted mulberry tree. Its branches were laden with ruby red fruits that shone like jewels as the suns rays caught their juicy flesh. I had imagined to be greeted by a dirty white lime washed cottage with a terracotta roof missing a few tiles, weathered blue shutters hanging from their hinges against the window frames and a garden strewn with lobster pots and sea buoy's. But it was nothing like I had imagined. It was quite the opposite.

"We can't possibly be staying here, could we? I thought he said it was going to be a traditional and simple? This is absolutely bloody gorgeous!" Sam said as we followed the pathway around the property and onto the sun terrace.

I couldn't even bring myself to speak. Stood between two white pillars that supported the overhanding roof above the large sun terrace, I stared straight out over the brightest turquoise sea I had ever seen. Its colour flooded my vision in every direction I looked and made me instantly calm. The land in front of the villa was filled with sage, thyme and rosemary that wafted their intoxicating citrusy scents on the warm breeze. The intensity of the yellow Spanish Broom flowers dotted the verdant landscape with a splash of vibrant colour. The land gradually rolled out of view towards the calm clear waters of a secluded beach below.

It oozed tranquillity and charm. I couldn't hear anything but the sound of the waves gently caressing the pebbles on the empty shores below and the frantic chirping of the swallows as they darted across the garden, scooping up an occasional drink of water from the small swimming pool that was sunk into the perfectly kept lawn. It was almost as if someone had painted the landscape before me. It was too magical to be real.

"This is absolutely breath taking!" I said as Elias unlocked the doors behind me.

"It is pretty no? Papa bought the old farm cottage and land here, then built the main house looking out over the sea. The original cottage and stables are just a few metres away and we sometimes have guests in them, but this has always been for family only and the occasional friends to enjoy. Papa, he no longer wanted to be here alone when my Mama died. So he moved in with my oldest brother and his family in the village. I come up here for a swim and to stay if I am late at the taverna. My home is in Argostoli, not far but it is much easier to be here for work sometimes in the summer months. The beach in front is very secluded and there is a hidden pathway in amongst the broom that will take you to the sea. If you are wanting to party, Spartia is not the place for all night dancing and drinking. Here we like a quiet life. In Skala, Argostoli and Lassi, you can find good nightlife. If you like history you must visit in the north to Fiscardo, Assos and Sami. Here are the keys, I hope that you will be comfortable and if you need anything please just visit with me at the taverna!" and with that he said his goodbyes and left.

Taking in one last deep breath of the calm sea air, I grabbed my suitcase and followed Julie and Sam inside the villa.

"Bagsy the double bed!" announced Julie as she marched on ahead to find her room.

The main living space was spacious and open plan with two large welcoming settees scattered with plumped cushions in a variety of bright colours positioned in front of a log burner. A large farmhouse style dining table filled the centre of a very modern white kitchen with all the electrical appliances you could need on display around the counter tops. Everything was freshly painted, spotlessly clean and the large windows brought in so much light from outdoors, giving it a very calm feeling. I could quite happily have lived in this house with no problems at all.

Passing by an open door, I could hear Julie singing away to herself as she placed the contents of her suitcase onto a bundle of hangers that were strewn across the bed. She had already changed into a beautiful flowing summer dress and looked as if she had literally just stepped out of a catalogue. Sam had found her room and replaced her suit with a skin-tight pair of Lycra shorts and baggy T shirt over her bikini.

Eventually finding an unoccupied room at the rear of the villa, I placed my suitcase down on the bed. The room was pleasantly decorated in a cooling shade of lavender blue and the bed freshly made with crisp white linen. A single dark wooden framed bed, a bedside table and a matching dressing table, were the only items of furniture in the room. A large built in wardrobe, with enough room for my entire winter and summer clothing collection, filled the wall next to the bedroom door.

A set of wooden French doors next to the bed, led out to a shaded sun terrace to the side of the villa. I threw open the doors and let a warm breeze into the coolness of the room. The area was completely secluded from the view of the neighbours by a thick bush of pine and olive trees. The delicate flowers from a jasmine plant, that had entwined itself around a wooden trellis attached to the villa wall, filled the air with its intoxicating aroma, creating a thick frame of foliage around the glass doors. Tucked into the furthest corner of the terrace was a small mosaic bistro table set with two matching chairs. Bathed completely in sun and hidden from the rest of the garden by a large fig tree, it looked like the perfect place to enjoy and afternoon nap. Just as my mind was drifting away with the gentle swaying of the surrounding shrubbery, Julie and Sam appeared around the door.

"Right then sweetie, are we ready to leave yet? Sammie dear you can't wear those shorts that high on your waist, it looks like your vagina is trying to eat them! Oh come on Lizzie, darling, I thought you would have unpacked and been ready to go by now! I can hear the wine list calling me from here!"

Sam stared down at her crotch and pulled her shorts a little lower onto her hips.

"That's much better Sammie, the locals would have though that they were on safari with you wandering around like that! Don't forget to pack your cossie and a towel! We can have a few dreamy hours on the beach after lunch. We will be waiting by the pool Lizzie. Don't be much longer as I am parched!"

"Do we have to go out straight away? Can't we just laze around for a few hours here and then go out later? I could do with an afternoon nap in the sun and a swim! I said, hoping that we could just stay in this little bit of Greek paradise.

"We need to find our bearings first. Work out where we are in relation to the rest of civilisation. We also need to buy some water to drink. Plus it is almost lunchtime and I am starving. Plenty of time for doing nothing!" Sam said like a sergeant major organising his troops.

"We have plenty of water in the taps! Why do we need to buy water?" I said feeling slightly confused.
"Because its what us Brits do wherever we go, Lizzie darling! Anyway, who knows how sophisticated the mains water supply is on this primitive island. It might just come straight from a mountain stream, which the local wildlife also drinks from and shits in!"

My nose scrunched up at the thought, but I could also have quite happily crashed out on the sun lounger in the serenity of our surroundings. Who knew you couldn't just drink from the tap like back home. Seems a little silly to me to be buying water in plastic bottles when there's a perfectly good source running straight into the villa. I bet, unknown to Julie, the local cafes and restaurants used the water straight from the tap. Maybe that was their secret to a youthful complexion.

Unzipping my suitcase, I slipped out of my travel clothes, replacing them with a flowing summer dress that I had bought from Marks and Sparks. As I lifted the dress over my head, the faint smell of pasties wafted from my armpits, which made me recoil a little. I could really have done with a shower but instead I gave them a fresh squirt of deodorant and hoped that would keep me going for a few more hours until I could give myself a swill in the salty sea. Giving my hair a ruffle and applying my Revlon Ultra lipstick in a light coral to match my aging skin tones and thinning lips, as sold to me by the beautician on the makeup counter in Debenhams, I headed out to join the girls.

Chapter 9

The walk back down to the taverna was long, hot and gruelling. The sun was now at its most intense, and the wind was almost as hot as my hairdryer. But even though the weather app on my phone told me it was nearing 38 degrees, it still felt much more comfortable than the occasional two-day heat waves that I had experienced back in London. Here at least, the heat felt natural against the wild landscape and not as uncomfortable as the intensified heat from the towering concrete blocks that acted like giant radiators making the city literally feel on fire.

We were only halfway to the taverna when a lizard big enough to make into a designer pair of shoes slinked across the hot tarmac in front of us. Almost sensing my fear, it stopped to examine our presence before disappearing into the sun-scorched undergrowth. Did it not know that my bladder is no longer capable of dealing with unexpected frights without prior warning? Gone were the days that I can concentrate on more than one thing. It is either mind over matter or mind over bladder. This time matter won, and I was grateful again for the discreetness of my Tenna Ladies. As we continued to navigate our way along the windy narrow road, the lushness of the eucalyptus, olive and endless pine trees gave a welcome shade from the unforgiving sun. Passing by a scattering of sleepy houses hidden from prying eyes by their blossoming verdant gardens, I caught my first glimmer of civilisation.

The road had abruptly ended at a small concrete jetty with a car park to the left shaded by a magnificent sheer white cliff that loomed above and hugged the coast for a few hundred meters before disappearing around the peninsular. The clinks of a few sailing boats could be heard as they moored in the harbour and sleepily bobbed about in the gentle swell. A scattering of towels and parasols covered the narrow stretch of sand. A few children played in the shallows watched over by relaxed parents. A cluster of swimmers had adventured out deeper into the clear blue bay and were leisurely swimming laps parallel to the sandy shore. It was as if time had completely slowed down, and everything had suddenly become so dreamy.

We found our way to the Waterway Café Bar and were greeted by a smiling Elias, who wandered over to show us to a shaded table that overlooked the bay.

"Kalo Mina ladies! I hope that you have made yourselves comfortable at the villa. Could I get you a drink whilst you make your choice from the menu? I can highly recommend the lobster that was caught fresh by my brother this morning from his boat, and to start, the stuffed peppers are superb! The feta is from our own goats here in Spartia."

"Efharisto, Elias." Sam said, giving him a courteous smile and continuing," The villa is just beautiful, and we are really so grateful that you could help us out of our sticky situation."

"Right then, ladies, let's get the party started the way it should have been! Can we order Sex on the Beach and a screaming orgasm, each please sweetie?" smiled Julie as Sam gave her a hard kick from under the table.

"Owww! What was that for? It's just a drink, darling Sammie! Sorry about her. She obviously has no sense of humour!"

Julie casually took a cigarette from its packet and asked a perplexed Elias politely for a light.

As he searched his pockets for a lighter, Julie placed the filter into her perfect Botox pout and sucked hard at the flame from the lighter that he held in his large masculine hand. As the cigarette began to glow a burning orange, Julie sat back in her chair, crossing her legs and exposing her flesh to the upper thigh before exhaling a perfect smoke ring. The whole time she did not take her eyes off poor Elias. It was like watching a cheesy 80's film starring a desperate middle-aged woman. She had already started her pursuit, and this was literally the second man that she had met on the island that day. As Elias disappeared towards the bar to pour our drinks, Julie noted us staring at her in complete silence.

"What? Oh, come on, darlings relax, it was just a bit of fun. He must have had so many other women tourists throwing them selves at him and asking him for the same drinks! He is pretty gorgeous isn't he? It's all part of being a Greek taverna owner. They all love it, you know!"

"But I don't love it, Julie. It's almost as if you are desperate for attention. Can't you just be normal like us?"

"Boring, don't you mean Sammie! You are so uptight! When was the last time you actually had sex with someone and not your vibrator? Your problem is you put them off with your feminism and icy barriers because you are scared of actually enjoying your self. Look at those wrinkles coming. You need to get married before you get to look too old! And if you can't find a husband, then maybe what you need is a good seeing to just to relax you a bit before your hole closes up for good!"

"Christ Julie, you are so crass! My wrinkles are all from laughing so much and having fun. Apart from the wrinkles between my eyes. They are my "what the fuck" lines from everything I see you doing or saying. Those wrinkles are very deep and all your fault! I am not going to throw myself at anyone because you think I have passed my prime. I don't want people thinking that I am as desperate as you! I am actually quite happy alone and in my own company. Just because I don't have a man it does not mean I want one, and I don't owe you any explanation as to why. We don't all need a man around to feel like a woman!"

As if someone had flicked a switch, I felt my face heat up in frustration. This was supposed to be a relaxing, enjoyable holiday and not a reminder of the family camping trips that always ended up with the children fighting. I went from completely calm and relaxed to psycho angry in a split second. It was almost as if I had been possessed by some kind of demon.

"Stop bickering, you two! It's like being on holiday with a fucking serial bride and a nun! For one, I actually wanted to get away from men for one good reason but each to their own. Sam, we both know that Julie is a bit of an arsehole at times," I said staring at Sam. "And Julie sometimes you need to consider others' feelings before blurting things out like some kind of verbal diarrhoea. If you think that I will spend the week being a referee, you can think again! This is our first day, and it has already been exhausting. Now both of you apologise and let us talk about something other than sex and men!!"

There was a moment of welcome silence for a while as we all sat back and took in the spectacular views across the bay. It didn't last long as Julie always had to have the last word.

"Christ! It's like being with a chronically depressed budgie being with you Sam. Cheer up for Gods sake, Sweetie!"

Sam scowled, thrust out her tongue and refrained from retaliating to her comment.

Spartia was a pretty resort with very little in the way of tourist development, which was partly why I had chosen it. Apart from a smaller restaurant at the top of the hill, The Waterway was the only place that you could enjoy a drink or meal overlooking the narrow sandy shores of Klimatsias beach.

The taverna was relaxing and welcoming. It was built into the hillside amphitheatrically and set out in various terraced levels, almost echoing the natural geology of the surrounding landscape. A blanket of triangular sails hypnotically flapped about in the gentle sea breeze high above our heads, giving a pleasant shelter from the hot summer sun. The sounds of traditional Greek bouzouki drifted across the airwaves amplifying the already mellow atmosphere. Its coastal location offered striking views over the infinite blues of the Ionian and was exactly how I had imagined a Greek taverna to be.

A pretty young waitress returned with our cocktails and politely took our food orders.

Taking the pink plastic stirrer in between her perfectly groomed fingertips, Julie gently stirred her drink, creating a satisfying crackle of ice against the tall glass. She removed the paper umbrella from the sugared rim and lifted the straw to her mouth. Taking a decent mouthful, she threw her head back, closed her eyes and let out a groan of complete satisfaction.

"Ughhhh!! God, I needed that! So darlings, what is our plan for this week? Do we have a schedule, or are we just going to freewheel for the entire holiday?"

"Well, I have been reading up a little on the island and its history. It's quite fascinating actually. Did you know that some believe this small island was named after the mythical persona of King Kefalos?"

"How droll, Sammie! Is that really how you please yourself? Does it really matter about it's past? All that matters is what it has to offer now, and from what I see, it really doesn't have a lot going for it. Just look at everyone on the beach. It's like being on a retirement holiday for the seven dwarves. Shall I point them all out for you?"

Julie stood and leaned forward across the table to get a better view of the beach below. Then, without a care who could hear her, she thrust her arm out and pointed her finger at her targets like an air rifle.

"Look!! There is Nappy, Wrinkly, Squinty, Rocky, Saggy, Farty and Leaky! There's not one adult on that beach that still has control of their bodily functions. If that woman's breasts sag any further, she will need another pair of flip flops to stop them dragging on the floor."

It felt as if the entire tavern had become quiet, and every diner was staring at us in complete shock at what had come out of Julie's mouth. I could have sunk under the table at that moment and hid away for the afternoon. Why Julie always took it upon herself to create a scene? It was as if she found some enjoyment in belittling others. Maybe getting old actually scared her as she had always depended on her looks to attract a man. I guess she was in denial that she was actually aging no matter what she did to make her body appear younger. She had spent thousands on getting her body to look twenty years younger and needed the lecherous stares of men to make it all feel worthwhile.

"Sorry about my friend. It's the menopause. It's turned her into a bit of an arsehole," I said rolling my eyes and apologising to the old lady that was sat at the table next to us. She nodded as if she completely understood exactly what I meant.

"Stop telling everyone that I am an arsehole. I like to see the look on their faces when they find out for themselves!" Julie sulked at me as she took another sip of her cocktail.

I looked around and noted that the majority of people were of retirement age, but I quite liked it. In fact, being around older people made me feel even more relaxed and body confident as I realised that I looked quite perky and youthful in comparison. There was not a perfect body insight, and I was glad of that.

In actual fact I was probably all of the dwarves in one with the way my body and mind were constantly changing. One minute I was itchy, then bitchy, sleepy, sweaty, bloaty, forgetful and psycho! Who knew which dwarf I would be

67

from one moment to the next. So I was more than content with my surroundings.

"Well I actually believe that the more you get to know about a place, the more you connect with it. If that educates me and makes me understand the locals better, then yes, I find pleasure in it. Anyway, I think you will like the story as it is about something you are familiar with....infidelity. Now let me educate your one-track mind."

Sam paused for a moment and took a sip of her drink through the straw before continuing.

"Apparently Kefalos was tricked into believing his wife was having an affair by a goddess who wanted him herself. She manipulated him into testing his wife's fidelity by disguising himself as another man and seducing her with expensive gifts. To his horror, his wife gave in to her secret admirer. Finding out it had been her king all along, the guilt of her betrayal made her flee to Crete where she hid for a while before returning to Athens to win back her husband from the goddess."

"Well, that's where we differ, darling! I would never have gone back to chase after him. She should have divorced him and taken his money!"

"I was referring more to the goddess who manipulated him into believing his wife was betraying him just so she could have him for herself, Jules!" Sam said, glaring disapprovingly across the table.

"Now where was I? Okay...Whilst Kefalos was out hunting, he saw a movement from behind a tree. Aiming his arrow, he shot at what he believed was prey. On approaching his kill, he was horrified to see that it was actually his wife that he had murdered by mistake. In his despair, he fled Athens and met up with the son of King Alcaeus, Amphitryon, who was on a revenge quest to gain the hand in marriage of his future wife, Alcmene. Helping his new acquaintance to defeat his rivals in battle, he was rewarded with this island, which he named Kefalonia! How cool is that!"

I loved hearing Sam speak about the history of the island. She had a thirst for knowledge and seemed to really soak up everything around her, almost like a sponge. Maybe that is why she had been so successful in her career. I bet she had swallowed a whole history book about the island as soon as we had booked our flight. I didn't mind, though, as it fuelled my romantic imagination. I could almost visualise the mighty Greek warriors battling it out on the shores of the island, all for the love of a woman.

Chapter 10

Having satisfied my hunger on a feast of stuffed vine leaves, fresh Greek salad, and local grilled fish, we had paid our bill and retreated to a quiet spot on the beach.

"Slap on the factor 50, darlings. None of us can afford any more wrinkles. Greeks never crease, you know. It's all the olive oil and donkey milk that keeps them looking so young," Julie had advised as we lay out our towels and stripped into our swimwear. I possibly needed to bathe in it for a few weeks for it to reverse the damage my lifestyle had already done to my skin.

My choice of bathing suit was a little more reserved, whilst Sam was happy to wear a tankini showing off her defined abs and long toned legs. Julie, on the other hand, had stripped down to a thong. Her recently enhanced pert breasts were in full view of the entire beach as she chanted away and did a few yoga stretches on the sand to the delight of the passing fishermen. I could tell some of the other women on the beach were not happy with her brashness. I can't say I blame them. From a distance, she did look like a supermodel in her twenties but close up, you could tell she was just mutton dressed as lamb. In actual fact, in the philosophy of Zen, we are all just molecules rushing through space and time. This means that there is no actual difference between me, the grains of sand between my toes, a goat, and Kylie Minogue, all apart from the obvious difference in the size of my bottom, of course.

The rest of the afternoon was spent lazing in the hot sunshine on the soft golden sand with the occasional dip in the astonishing warm waters of the Ionian Sea. This was a long way from the cold, dirty brown seas I was used to off Clacton beach. There I feared what was lurking under the surface as my feet disappeared into its salty, muddy murkiness. It wasn't the thought of a shark attack that worried me. It was more likely that a brown turd or used sanitary towel floated past as I took a swim.

Here the water almost seduced you into its depths with its different gradients of blue. My mind went through the colour spectrums from vivid turquoise to a cerulean blue to cobalt, then navy as it met with the sky blues of the cloudless horizon. As I swam across the crystal clear waters, small shoals of silverfish caught the sun's rays as they darted underneath me to the safety of the slightly pink coral-covered rocks below. Who knew marine life was so beautiful. Apart from watching an episode of David Attenborough's "The Living Planet" on the TV or visiting an aquarium, I had never been surrounded by marine creatures in their natural habitat.

It made me wonder what it would be like to submerge myself into their silent world even more. Taking a deep breath, I dipped my head and dived below the surface towards the seabed. I could see just a blur of endless blue everywhere I turned and could hear nothing but my heart that seemed to beat with the sounds of the waves and swell of the tide. It was so peaceful that I could have listened to it for much longer had I not suddenly felt a gripping tightness in my chest. My head began to pound as if it was going to explode, then my heart sped up with the urgent need for oxygen. In a panic, I thrust myself upwards like a torpedo off a large rock under my feet, towards the liquid brightness above, breaking through the surface just in time. Taking in a welcoming gasp of the warm afternoon air, I reminded myself that, although I would have liked to consider myself like the Disney mermaid princess, Ariel, I was actually more like Moby Dick.

Tiring of the sun, we wandered back into the taverna to call a taxi which arrived in no time and took us to the nearby town to get a few essentials from the only supermarket in the village, Marina's. Having picked up everything we needed and indulging in an inflatable pink flamingo for the pool, we found the taxi driver enjoying a coffee in the adjoining bar. Asking if we were in a rush, he suggested that we joined him for a refreshingly cold pina colada cocktail. He was a jovial man in his late sixties. His deep olive skin still seemed so youthful for his age. He joked that this was due to the magic of the Kefalonian olive oil and fresh goat's milk, which prevented wrinkles. Julie laughed and gave us the" told you so" look.

The village itself was small and very quiet. The narrow streets were filled with flowering shrubs and sprawling trees, making it feel like part of the surrounding landscape. Traditional homes happily coexisted next to the few holiday villas and small hotels in the village, making tourists instantly feel a part of the community.

Having happily chatted for a while and finished our drinks, the taxi driver dropped us back at the villa. We arranged for him to return at around 8pm to take us back to the beach for our evening meal. This gave us just enough time to enjoy a shower each and have a glass of wine on the sun terrace. There was an evening of Greek entertainment lined up at the taverna, and I was looking forward to enjoying a relaxing night filled with good food and the sounds of Greece in the background as the sunset golden over the sea. But the reality of it was that I was with Sam and Julie, so I knew it would not be so idyllic.

As we wandered up the steps of the taverna, a young waiter showed us to a lovely table on a small grassy area that overlooked the beach. The setting sun sent countless hues of reds, purples, and blues across the entire bay. My eyes were plunged into the infinite watery horizon before being drawn towards the limestone cliffs that had been illuminated pink by the parting sun. The laughter of a few children could be heard as they bathed in the crystal clear shallows as twilight arrived. A few stray cats all lazed about in the grass surrounding the tables, waiting for any titbits to fall to the floor for them to scavenge.

"Sweetie, before you disappear, would you be so kind as to take a photograph of the three of us together, with the sun setting behind us?" Julie said as she handed the waiter her telephone and gave him a quick demonstration of how to use the camera.

"No problem! If you could all stand close together and smile!"

"Wait! Wait! We need to get ready! Right darling's, grab the back of each other's necks, and after three, pinch hard! Trust me, it will give us all an instant jaw lift!
One...Two...Three...Go!! Say Cheese!"

The camera flash sent a sudden brightness across the dusky sky.

"Let me check just in case we look ghastly, and you need to do it again! Let me see!" she said as she quickly checked his handwork. "Perfect, thank you, sweetie. Could I order a Gin Sling for myself?"

"A double vodka on the rocks for me!" Sam piped in.

"A carafe of house red for me, please," I added as the waiter disappeared into the bar.

Julie flicked through her mobile and sent a copy of the photo beeping to our own phones within a few seconds. She wasn't wrong, you know! That pinch had given me back at least ten years of my life!

The restaurant was beginning to fill up, and for a few hours, we chatted away and enjoyed each other's company without as much as a snide remark or crudity from either Sam or Julie.

I had never really tried Greek cuisine before. Not unless you counted a kebab that I often devoured after a drunken night out in the city to soak up the copious amounts of alcohol I had consumed in my teens. But it almost always ended up being thrown up over a garden wall as I emptied the contents of my stomach and staggered my way home to my bed as the sun began to rise. Nothing tastes great after you have vomited.

But the food really surpassed my expectations, and the greasy kebab vomit experience was long forgotten. How had I never eaten Greek food before? The intense aroma of cinnamon, rosemary, thyme, onions, and garlic mixed with the sweetness of tomatoes and chargrilled meats filled the night air. I had settled on the stuffed peppers as a starter and a traditional meat pie, Kreatopita, as my main course.

74

Neither meal disappointed. As I bit into the sweetness of the roasted peppers, the creamy feta and olive oil oozed out and drizzled down my chin. It was one of the most satisfying starters that I had ever tasted and had left me wanting more. My mouth had already started to salivate when the main course was placed in front of me. That was even before I had cut into the golden flakes of the crispy filo pastry. The pie was packed with rice, meat, and tomatoes infused with traditional wild herbs that made it sweet and smoky at the same time. Every mouthful was orgasmic. I could hardly move after moping up the remains with a piece of warm home-baked bread. Skipping on the offer of a dessert, the waiter returned with a shot of the local liqueur, Matsika.

Explaining that it was a magical drink from the ancients that would bring us good health and luck, Julie and Sam knocked it back instantly, while I was more cautious and decided to just take a few occasional sips. The flavour was hard to describe. The first taste was a bit like a mixture of slightly minted toothpaste with a hit of one of those organic pine-scented toilet-cleaning products. Then the second taste was almost like chewing a tree bark dipped in honey. And my final taste was more floral, a bit like an aromatherapy incense stick. It was most definitely magical if it tasted different on every sip!

As the waiter cleared our table and took our drinks order, a group of young lads that had been setting up a few microphones and a set of drums on one of the terraces began to play. One of the lads started to strum away at a small decorative egg-shaped guitar that Sam pointed out to be a bouzouki. The strings' low metallic sound vibrated through the air, almost creating a humming noise that tuned in with the beat of your heart as he strummed out a virtuosic melody. The melody started off slow and mellow, almost as relaxing as the pace of life in this sleepy little fishing village. As it gradually picked up speed, the tune became more urgent and chaotic yet remaining very uplifting and jovial. It sent a rush of goosebumps down my arms causing the hairs to stand on end.

A group of male folk dancers wearing traditional Greek peasant clothing burst out from the inside of the taverna. They were all linked from shoulder to shoulder, creating a continuous chain. They began to dance in time with the music in complete synchronisation, forming an ever-moving circle. I found the dancing to be quite intense, almost as if the men were portraying their masculinity. If they were, it was working as I was finding it quite sexy. I became hypnotised by their ability to keep their upper body entirely still while swaying their lower half with the occasional bounce or spring to their complicated foot movements. The music had created a ripple of excitement as the diners clapped in time with the music.

An entire family of Greeks had filled a few of the tables on the tier above us. They were really getting into the spirit of things. There must have been every generation of the family out that night, including the couple that we had gatecrashed earlier that morning. Swarms of children were all running around the table in circles. Some had left the taverna to play on the beach. The parents were chattering away and not at all concerned about the absence of their children. It was such a different family way of life. I watched as the group of children skimmed pebbles across the surface of the sea and playfully chased each other with seaweed. There was not a mobile phone in sight which was quite unusual considering they all ranged in age from about seven up to sixteen.

I looked out across the horizon where the brightness of the moon was now illuminating the tips of the waves in the distance. The sky above was filled with the twinkling stars that shone so bright in the complete darkness. The stray cats, now full from their foraged meals, happily lay on the surrounding walls and groomed their fur under the milky moonlight. Cicadas chirped their evening song in the surrounding wild herbs, which saturated the night air with heady pine-like aromas. An occasional goat bleat could be heard echoing from the fields above. This was the most relaxed I had felt in a long time.

By 11pm, many of the other diners had left for the night, and only a few tables remained. One of the Greek women came to speak to us and introduced herself as Maria. She insisted that we should join their family celebrations. Her Papou, Costas, was celebrating his 100th birthday, so the night was still young. Out of sheer politeness, we accepted their kind offer and took a seat amongst their vast family. Julie found a seat next to a very distinguished middle-aged man and was deep in conversation. I was placed next to the sweetest-looking Greek lady who must have been at least ninety and spoke no English. She just smiled and nodded at me every now and again. Sam, who was already a little tipsy, apologised profusely at the young couple she had chased around the pool that morning.

What I had actually observed from this experience is that Greeks have two volumes. Loud and louder! The language was rapid and very animated. If I had not seen some of the other family members laughing at the exchanges between each other, I would have believed that they were arguing. They also didn't stop eating as different food dishes were spread out across the length of the table, which people seemed to continuously snack on. They also drink like a fish, without it seeming to affect them at all. The waiters were continually clearing empty glasses and returning with another tray of shots. By the fourth shot of ouzo, I had started to feel a little lightheaded. But the drinks kept coming, and after every shot, we sank, the entire table would raise their empty glass above their heads and shout Opa!! For a while, I thought it was the waiter's name, as he seemed to appear with more drinks each time it was shouted.

Occasionally I would catch a glimpse of Elias smiling at me from behind the bar. At first, I thought he was smiling at the beautiful young woman that had been sat to my left until I noted that she had moved seats and I was utterly alone. One of the men was chattering away to me across the table about his son's company that did tourist excursions in the mountains. I could hardly understand what he was saying, but I nodded my head in agreement and acted as if I knew what he was on about.

As the entire family erupted into a song, I looked around, trying to keep tabs on the girls. I had completely lost sight of Julie, who was now nowhere to be found, and Sam was chatting to the barmaid, leaving me completely alone with the Greek version of the Von Trappes. Then, totally against my better judgment, I was encouraged to join in with the Greek dancing. The music had started off very slow, which I could keep up with, but then the pace quickened, and my little legs found it almost impossible to keep up. My coordination was a little impaired due to the amount of alcohol I had consumed, and with all the jiggling about, my strapless bra was not as supportive as I had needed it to be right at that moment.

78

I don't know how many times I had charged around in the circle before I looked down and noticed my very large left boob fully exposed and bouncing about to the beat of the music. The last thing I remembered was stepping into the centre of the circle to try to make myself decent and hoping nobody had seen my embarrassing wardrobe fail. The dancers' speed and intensity spinning around me made me feel like I was part of some strange cult, and I was about to be sacrificed. The amount of alcohol I had consumed mixed with a hot flush from hell made me feel lightheaded and dizzy. The whole universe appeared to be spinning around. Then, the entire world became black, and I hit the floor.

Chapter 11

It must have been after midday when I eventually opened my eyes. My head hurt, and I could hardly lift it off the pillow. I wasn't sure if the room was actually hot or my body was creating its own tropical climate again. Everywhere ached, my mouth was as dry as a flipflop, and I needed cool air. I also needed a strong coffee so that I could function. Pushing myself up reluctantly from my bed, I stretched upwards. Every bone in my body crunched and clicked back into place. Slowly, I shuffled my way towards the French doors and threw open the curtains. My entire body recoiled at the unwelcome brightness of the day.

Pushing open the heavy glass doors, hoping for a fresh breeze to cool me down, I was presented with an even hotter blast of air. I should have been happy about the perfect weather that greeted me, but the thing about getting drunk is it borrows your happiness from the following day. I hadn't been drunk in a long time, and now I was regretting it.

The warm breeze also brought with it the intense aroma of the jasmine flowers that framed the doorway. At any other time, I would have been delighted by their flora inception. But that morning, the heady scent was just too much for me to cope with and turned my stomach. I rushed to the bathroom just in enough time to vomit the contents of the night before into the toilet bowl.

Eventually, after managing to get myself up off the floor, I stared at myself in the mirror. My own reflection was enough to make me recoil in horror. I was so glad that there was nobody else around to see the state I was in. I looked like a mummified Red Indian. My hair was stuck up everywhere and had some kind of food substance gluing it to the side of my head. My eyes sagged down my face and were like pinholes under the puffiness of my eyelids. Mascara and lipstick had smudged all over my cheeks. What the hell had happened last night?

I headed to the kitchen to make that much-needed coffee before I even considered making myself feel human again.

"Christ! You look like I need a drink! What the hell happened to you last night?" Sam said from where she stood by the open door that led out of the villa towards the pool.

"Creeping Jesus! Did you have to sneak up on me?" I said as I jumped at least a foot in the air with fright. "I was going to ask you if you knew Sam! I have no clue. All I remember is one minute being surrounded by dancers, and the next thing, everything went black. How the hell did we get home, and where is Julie?"

"Can't help you there! I got back this morning, and you were flat out, so I left you to sleep it off. Julie's bed is not slept in, so I guess she never came home."

"So where the hell is she? Have you tried her mobile? And where the hell did you stay last night?" I said as I flicked on the kettle.

"No idea where she could be. Her mobile is going straight to the answerphone, and I have sent her a text message, which she hasn't yet answered. She is possibly under some wealthy Greek on his million-pound yacht as we speak. You know what she is like. She will be fine." Sam reminded me. "I, um, I met someone, and all I can say is I had a great time," Sam said, smiling smugly at me like a teenager after their first kiss.

The sensible Mum mode had stepped in, and as the kettle boiled away, I found my hands levitate to my hips, and my head shake automatically from side to side. As I realised what I was doing, I wondered exactly how many tragedies I had prevented by standing in this exact pose over the years as those pearls of wisdom came so naturally from my mouth.

"You should be more careful just staying out with any Tom, Dick, or Harry. Anything could have happened to you, and I would have had no clue where you were! It is bad enough we have Julie to contend with. I don't expect that behaviour from you! You are old and wise enough to know better!"

"It was Elly actually, not Tom, Dick, or Harry" Sam smiled as she took a sip of her drink.

My mouth must have been wide open, as I had no words at that moment. I had always thought that she was just too busy with work for men. It had never occurred to me that she was actually a lesbian.

"Don't look so shocked, Lizzie! You must have noticed that having known me for all these years. You, of all people I thought would have guessed by the way that I stare at women and don't take any notice of men. My personal trainer is gay and he has helped me with my feelings along the way. A bit like a sexual therapist as well as a damn good fitness trainer. I also got to meet a few girlfriends with his help. The women that you saw me with weren't clients, they were my dates. Julie is so pre-occupied with herself that she really has no time to notice what is going on with anyone else's life. I can't believe that it has taken me until I am almost fifty to actually come out with the fact that I am gay."

My foggy mind could not absorb what I was being told. Don't get me wrong, I have no problems with anyone's sexuality. At the end of the day, love is love no matter where it comes from. At least she was happy and getting laid. Even though I joked about being happy single, the fact was I wasn't. I was so used to being with a man that I felt that I had to have one in my life. I had begun to think that I would never experience that feeling again in my entire life. Who would want an overweight middle-aged dried-up woman anyway?

Finding a moment's relief from the heat in the coldness of the fridge, I took out the milk and splashed a little of the cold white liquid into my drink before heading out to join Sam on the patio.

"I am pleased for you, Sam. I really am. Just be careful, that's all! We are in a strange country, and I don't want you getting banged up. It's bad enough we have Julie gone AWOL on us. I couldn't cope if you went missing too!"

Sam leaned forward and grabbed hold of my hand in hers.

"Stop being that person, Lizzie. You need to give
yourself a break from being a parent. We are old enough
and ugly enough to deal with our own shit. You just
need to sort yourself out. It's time you found a little
happiness and adventure in your life. I am going to take a
swim to cool myself off before I check my emails.
Unfortunately, I can't just take time off as I need to earn
a living!" Sam got up from the table, took off her beach
wrap, and dived gracefully into the pool.

She was right. I couldn't drop the parenting act even
though my children had long left the nest. I had no clue
who else I was supposed to be. A knock at the door
brought me out of the moment. Thinking it might be
Julie, I rushed to answer. To my surprise, Elias stood in
complete shock at my unexpected appearance at the
doorway. I must have looked a right sight as I had totally
forgotten about the state I had woken up in.

"You are not ready to leave? You did say after lunch to
pick you up, no?" he smiled, looking me up and down.

I looked at him blankly and feeling quite confused.

"You not remember making plans for today. I brought
you home from the taverna last night after you fell. We
arranged to visit my old deserted family village in the
mountains. It's okay if you don't want to come. Maybe
another day!"

"Sorry, Elias. Last night is a little foggy for me. Too many
ouzo's! I really don't remember much at all but thank
you for bringing me home. I would love to come, but

Sam is here by herself, and I am not sure where Julie is. She didn't come home last night."

Sam shouted from behind me.

"Go! Go! I have work to be done here, so I will be busy all afternoon, and Julie is not your responsibility remember!"

"Are you sure you don't mind?"

"Not at all. Go and find your own adventures!"

"Give me a few minutes to sort myself out and get a few things together. I will be with you as quick as I can, Elias."

"Endaxi! I will be in the car!"

Feeling a little flustered about my lack of memory, I headed to the bathroom to grab a few essentials, spray on some deodorant and rub on an excess of sunscreen. Reminding myself over and over of Julie's advice, Greeks don't crease.

Looking a little more human, I popped my head out of the doorway, shouted my goodbyes to Sam, who was busy swimming laps of the pool as if she was training for the Olympics. Just watching her made me feel exhausted. I could only just find the energy to get out of bed that morning. I made my way out through the front door.

Elias was leaning on the bonnet of his car, busy texting away on his phone, when my sudden appearance made him jump a little.

"Sorry that I scared you twice already this morning! I hope that I am looking a little more presentable now," I smiled, fishing for compliments at my transformation from the undead to almost dead in a matter of minutes.

"I hope you are not going out of your way too much taking me out for the afternoon."

"Not at all. I enjoy getting up into the mountains for some air. It reminds me that we are the lucky ones who have not much to worry about. You look much better since you changed," he smiled. "Let me put your bag in the boot, and we will head upwards!"

Chapter 12

The hot mid-day sun burnt at my arm as it penetrated through the car window. I was glad for the air conditioning that sent an ice-cold breeze over my face as I sweated my way quietly through yet another hot flush.

Being in a car with a complete stranger was not easy for me. I had never done anything like this before and was not too sure that I was comfortable with it. We had been in the car for almost 5 minutes already, and neither of us had attempted to speak. I had no clue whether I should start a conversation or not. I also had no idea what to say. Stating the obvious about the weather seemed a little too British. Instead, I studied the scenery in silence and absorbed the serenity of my surroundings.

We wound our way upwards through switchback after switchback as the mountainous roads snaked endlessly ahead through the pine-covered hills. The composition of the landscape seemed to transform before my eyes with every turn in the road. From thick pine forests to thickets of wildflowers scattering the vista with bursts of colour and then the harsh scrub that rolled down towards the coast, which drifted further into the distance as we continued to climb. Until just a faint glisten from the sun twinkled on the horizon as it caressed the cerulean and turquoise sea.

We passed by a few goats that had made themselves comfortable on the hot tarmac of the main road and seemed unfazed by the occasional car or lorry that trundled past. A few weathered cottages occasionally whizzed by as we drove through small mountain villages that appeared to have been lost with time. I had not seen another person from the moment we left Spartia.

"So, why did you choose to come to the island?" Elias said, breaking the silence.

"I just needed to get away from my old life for a while. Kefalonia looked like a great place to relax and spend some time with my friends."

"Your friend, the blonde one, she is a bit crazy, no?"

"Julie. Yes. She is a bit of a character. Her bite is worse than her bark if you fall for her, and most men do. We have all been friends since we were small, so I know how to cope with her antics. She has this habit of acting like a lone wolf occasionally and forgetting that we came as a group. God knows where she got to last night, and it worries me that she hasn't bothered to let us know she is okay. She probably hasn't even considered that she has put herself in danger. The trouble with her being so much trouble is that she doesn't know she is in trouble until she is in trouble. Do you know what I mean?"

"I have no clue what you mean!" Elias laughed. "Anyway, she is not my type of woman. She is too, how you say, in your face? She left with Dimitris last night. He owns a vineyard here. She is in no trouble with him. He will look after her just fine!"

"It's not her I am worried about it's him! Typical of her to sniff out a rich vineyard owner and have her own endless supply of wine. She is like a bloodhound, you know, trained to do exactly that." I said, rolling my eyes at my discovery.

"You have a caring side that makes you worry too much. That I like about you, but you must let her live her life, and you try to concentrate just on yours. She is a grown woman, and from what I saw, she can handle her own trouble" He smiled.

I smiled at his answer. Both he and Sam were right. But just deciding to stop caring was not that simple when it was all I knew.

"We are here!" he announced as we came to a stop next to a small pink church-like building. Beyond the tall Cypress pines, I could see the looming ruins of where an old church once had stood. Elias turned the engine off and stepped out of the car.

I stepped out of the car and into the heat of the sun. The air smelt like honey with a hint of wild fennel and sage. The sun was hot and unforgiving. Every now and then, I could hear the gentle sounds of a goat bell echoing across the valley. I followed Elias, who had already started to walk ahead towards a tall ruined tower.

"This was the kampanario, the bell tower, which would have called the villagers to the church service. It is now the only ruin that still stands complete in the village. There is a staircase inside, come!" he motioned as he disappeared inside the tower.

The ruin looked like it could crumble at any time. A giant crack ran deeply from top to bottom and gave me little faith that it would not collapse under my weight. Elias popped his head out of a small arched window located halfway up the tower.

"Are you coming? You can see everything from up here." He smiled as he pointed into the verdant density.

Reluctantly I wandered into the darkness of the tower. The thick walls smelt damp and decayed but gave a little coolness to the unforgiving heat outside. A small amount of light filtered in from above, just enough for me to navigate the stone spiral staircase that led upwards. I found my way towards the arched window. Poking my head through the opening, I looked out onto the dense leafy canopy that shrouded the landscape.

"Keep coming up. It is incredible up here but be careful of your step!" Elias echoed from above.

My fingers felt their way across the rough surface of the ancient stone as I hugged my large backside against the curve of the wall. Placing my feet cautiously onto each step, I continued to follow the narrow stairs, eventually seeing the welcome sight of Elias' legs at the opening to the roof.

"Take my hand. It is tiny up here for us both," he said, offering his hand downwards as he saw me emerge from the darkness below.

I was so grateful for his robust and reassuring grip. The top of the tower was completely exposed, with nothing to stop us from falling to our death below. It could not have been more than four feet wide in every direction. I was too scared to step out from the safety of the staircase just in case the walls crumbled from beneath my feet. Even though I was scared shitless, I felt a little like Rapunzel looking out for her prince over breathtaking views from her tall prison tower. It had an element of romance entwined with the undeniable sadness of the surroundings.

"Our family home was just over there beyond the walnut trees," he motioned as I followed his gaze towards a settlement of stone cottages that sat almost hidden amongst the overgrown vegetation.

Surrounded by the majestic mountains that dominated the landscape, the crumbling ruins were almost lost in the sprawling forests that had reclaimed the landscape. At first sight, it was not easy to recognise this as a village. But as I continued to follow his extended finger, I started to notice the crumbling walls and window voids that stared at me from out of the wilderness like hollow eyes watching over our uninvited intrusion.

Soon, it was easy to imagine the abandoned cobbled streets that would have once bustled with village life. I could almost hear the haunting sounds of a violin with its joyful uplifting tune, as people danced in celebration together along the cobbles. Now, fallen masonry engulfed by scrub was almost lost beneath the swathes of creeping ivy. Tree branches and brush broke out of crevices where windows and roofs would have once been. Carved lintels and architraves hinted at the prosperity the village had once enjoyed. Moss-covered steps led through rusted gates and into the lost homes of generations past.

Trailing behind Elias as he made his way back down the spiral staircase, we followed the sun-scorched trails deeper into the ruins. Stepping carefully over the wildflowers that carpeted the forgotten pathways, we followed the zig-zagged streets that led between the ruins. Mulberry and fig trees, ripe with their abundance of fruits, spilled out from forgotten gardens, gently returning them to a native wilderness.

Elias pointed out an old well where the villagers would have collected the fresh spring water that ran off the surrounding mountainsides. Ornate balustrades of Venetian architecture lay broken and strewn amongst the overgrown grasses that were littered with rusted tools—all remnants of a thriving mountain village that now sat silently in the shadows of the past. We continued our walk through the haunting streets until we reached a clearing that gave open views across to a thriving modern village.

"That is new Valsamata where the villagers from here fled and rebuilt their lives. There is a festival there every year in August to celebrate the Robola wine. It is a good festival with lots of drinking and dancing. I am sure you would enjoy after your dancing last night!' he laughed, reminding me of my previous night's antics.

I gave him a sheepish smile at the thought of what I must have looked like that morning when he arrived at my door.

"There are so many other abandoned villages like this on Kefalonia. So many beautiful buildings and homes are destroyed by nature. We all live with the knowledge that at any moment, the gods can claim back what is rightfully there's. Our island is very close to a fault line beneath the sea. We experience many earthquakes throughout our lives here. But I am lucky to have not yet lived through one as devastating as this," he said, turning to look back at the ruins.

We made our way back along the eerie pathways until we reached a small house on the outskirts of the village.

"This was my family's home!" Elias announced.

I took in the simplistic beauty of the humble building. The walls were now thickly carpeted by a Jasmine creeper that spilled out over a fragile wooden pagoda giving a little shade from the sun's intensity. A gentle warm zephyr stirred its verdant leaves, sending an intoxicating aroma of perfume into the air. A set of stone steps ran up the outside towards a small weathered door that led into the upper level. Stepping through the low doorway into the ruins' ground floor, I could just make out where the bedrooms would have been if the floors above were still in place. And old Aga sat rusting away against a crumbling ivy-clad wall in what would have once been a busy Greek kitchen.

As we stepped into the forgotten gardens, Elias pointed out an orchard of ancient twisted olive trees that generations of his family had once harvested. Clusters of cultivated flowers mixed in with native wild plants identified where an ornamental garden had once been tended. Large paddle-style scales and strawberry-shaped fruits of cacti poked out sporadically from the unruly overgrowth.

I bent forward and picked a pretty blue flower that filled an area against a crumbling wall, disturbing the stillness. A dozen large dragonflies darted out from the foliage below and filled the sky with a rainbow from their multi-coloured bodies that turned almost neon in the glimmering sun. Hovering above us like small helicopters, almost in protest of my rude disturbance, they finally retreated and found a warm spot on the surrounding stone walls. Placing the small bell-like flowers against my nose, I took in its sweet grape-like scent.

"This is Muscari. It is normally not this late to flower. My yiayia would harvest the bulbs for making winter soup. It was like the ambrosia of the gods in the chilly cold. But for the summer, she would pickle them to go with meats and salad," he stated as if eating flowers bulbs a usual way of life.

I had no clue of anything edible beyond the fresh vegetable aisle in the local supermarket. I had once grown a tomato plant by mistake when one had fallen from the table into our spider plant. It had produced a handful of juicy red fruit without any nurturing from myself. That was the extent of my green fingers. Reverting my thoughts back to my surroundings, I noted a stone grape and olive press that lay discarded amongst the brambles. It was evident that this had been his family's way of life for generations.

"How old is this place?" I questioned.

"A few hundred years probably," Elias answered.

"Has it been empty for long?" I wondered.

"A long time now since my Papa was a small boy. My family lived here until the earthquake in 1953 made it impossible for the villagers to return to their old lives. That's when this village was abandoned and rebuilt nearby." He said, returning his thoughts to the ghosts of his past surrounding him. "They lost their home and only source of income and lived in poverty for a long time after the disaster."

I couldn't find anything to say that would have felt right at that moment, so I stayed silent and just listened to the sound of the breeze as it stirred the surrounding vegetation. I took in the crumbling ruins that lay scattered all around. It was an eerie and forlorn sensation that was amplified by our sole presence. The amount of destruction was almost biblical yet peaceful as nature softly soothed away the pain of the past. There was nowhere quite like it back in the UK.

"Is it always this quiet?"

"Apart from people who come to tend the graves in the old churchyard, or the occasional tourist that stumbles across its existence. Yes, always. A bit like a shrine to our past!"

The only sound that could be heard was the urgent chatter of swallows as they darted through the ruins chasing their afternoon meal, the crickets that chirped away in the long grasses, and the occasional goat bleat that echoed across the valley from further up the mountain.

I could have explored the endless streets and ruins for hours, but the air was now so dry that it felt as those I had swallowed a mouthful of the dusty landscape. My lips were starting to feel chapped, and my skin felt tight from the lack of humidity. Elias turned, and, noting my tongue trying to return the moisture to my lips, he suggested that we start to make our way back to the car for a drink of water.

Passing through gates into the churchyard, I was surprised to see how neatly maintained the graves of lost ones were against the ruins that surrounded them. The churchyard was immaculate. A burst of colourful freshly arranged graced the white well-tended gravestones. Hurricane lanterns sat at the foot of the graves, ready to light up the darkness in their memory as pictures of the dead gave a reminder of their once physical existence on this very soil.

In the centre sat the ruins of what would once have been a magnificent church. The walls were now weathered with time, and parts of the render had fallen to the ground. Tufts of grass sprung out from the small crevices and cracks that had been caused by the earthquake. I stepped through the archway into what was left of the old church. A scattering of rubble covered the grassy floor where the church pews would have once been.

Even though I was surrounded by crumbling walls, I could feel the spiritual importance the building would have had to the villagers. I looked up at the deep blue skies above, and for a moment, I felt humble in my surroundings. It was almost as if I was being looked upon by something more significant than I could understand. Then, my stomach let out a massive deep grumble and alerted me that I needed to eat.

Chapter 13

I arrived back just after 4pm to an empty villa. Sam had left a note on the kitchen table to say that she had gone to the beach. I quickly checked Julie's room, but there was no sign that she returned from her night with Dimitris. I opened the fridge and took some olives, cheese, and a slice of baklava that I had bought the day previous. Then placing my snack on a plate and pouring myself a glass of freezing cold water, I headed into the bedroom to put on my swimsuit. A few hours lazing in the sun in complete silence would be the perfect way to spend the remainder of the afternoon.

After devouring my light snack, I cooled off in the pool for a while. It felt as though I had found my own perfect little bit of paradise. The colour of the sky, the sea, and the surrounding flowers actually made a big difference to my mental health. I felt a little more invigorated and ready for whatever old age was going to bring. The water gently lapped against my warm skin, and the lulling sound of the waves below had made me feel sleepy. Being a little refreshed from my swim, I pulled myself out of the pool and positioned one of the sun loungers into the sun.

Feeling confident that I was utterly alone for a while, at least, I slipped my swim costume off my shoulders and around my waist to expose my enormous naked bosoms. Plastering my entire body and face with SPF 50 to stop any unwanted additional wrinkles, I lay down and listened to the birds chirping away in the surrounding bushes. The sensation of the hot sunshine as it teased at my body and made my skin tingle with its welcome caress was a divine experience. There were no screaming children or demanding partners to disturb my peace. I could just lay there in complete selfishness and do absolutely nothing.

I must have dropped off almost instantly in the afternoon sun. I was rudely awoken by a piercing shriek from Julie, who had finally found her way home. She had found me out cold on my back with my breasts sagging under my armpits and a line of dribble rolling down my cheek.

"Jesus, Lizzie darling! I thought you were dead for a second! Cover yourself up before we get aircraft landing here from the colour on your breasts! Where is Sammie? I have arranged for us to go out for the night, and we are being picked up at seven," she announced as she lit a cigarette.

"What time is it? And where the hell did you end up last night? Did you not think that we would be a little worried about you considering your bed hadn't been slept in?" I replied as I noted the sunburn on my chest.

I pulled my swim costume back over my shoulders and felt a little sore from the sun regardless of the lashings of sunscreen that I had applied.

"Do you think that I am not gorgeous enough to look after myself? I have done a pretty fine job in control of my life over the past 30 years, without you getting concerned about my whereabouts. Now, it's almost six, and I am making tea. Would you like to join me?" she said as she wandered inside.

A little bemused by her choice of drinks, I waited for her to return. A few seconds later, Julie emerged from the kitchen and handed me a cold glass.

"What kind of tea is this?' I said, a little confused by the cubes of ice floating in clear liquid that she had passed me.

"It is tea, darling! As in Tea-quila!" she said as she threw her head back and let out a wicked laugh. "Get it down you. We aren't here for a long time. We are here for a good time!" she winked and necked back the contents of her glass in one.

"I am still trying to recover from last night, and after the hangover, I had this morning, I don't think I will be drinking for a while to come!" I announced as I handed her back the glass.

"You need to lighten up, Lizzie! Let your hair down and enjoy the day as if it is your last. What happened to you last night anyway, and where is Sammie?" she said as she knocked back my drink.

"I ended up getting drunk on ouzo with a bunch of complete strangers, dancing about like Stavros Flatley with my left breast bouncing about fully exposed to everyone in the taverna before passing out in a heap on the floor! Luckily Elias gave me a lift home as neither you nor Sam was anywhere to be seen!" I replied, feeling a little bit abandoned by my friends.

"Sounds like you had a ball!! Did you get any, you know what, when you got back, sweetie? She said as she thrust her hips back and forth between her clenched fists.

"God no!! I am so glad that part of my life is over. My plumbing is hard enough to maintain without complicating things. Elias was a complete gentleman and left immediately after getting me back safely, I think anyway," I said, aware that I actually remembered nothing about that part of the night. Anything could have happened when we arrived back and I wouldn't have been any wiser. But if it had I was gutted I hadn't been conscious enough to enjoy it!

"I know it's a sensitive subject to talk about, darling, but I can't believe the only man that you have ever slept with is Dave. You are not that bloody ugly, so what exactly is the matter with you. You need to brush away those cobwebs and get back out there while you are still lubricated enough! Elias is a pretty hot man for his age. Even if it is just to get back on the saddle again, you should join him for a ride. Hell, you might actually enjoy it! Don't let Dave be the only man that you have ever slept with. What a shame for your loins to never go Greek when they had the chance. I think I have tried every nationality known to man!" she said, taking another drag of her cigarette. "Where did you say Sammie had got to?"

"She is at the beach. I f you send a text and let her know what time we are going out, she will make her way back in time. I am not her mother, you know!" I announced as I pushed myself up from the lounger and wandered inside. "I am going to freshen myself up and get ready.

You take way too long in the shower. I am glad you are back safe, Jules!" I added as I shut the bathroom door. I gently peeled off my swimsuit and stepped into the shower. The warm spray initially stung like nettle rash against my reddened complexion. Turning the temperature down a little, I allowed the gentle spray to soothe my hot skin. I washed out the dirt from my hair that had blown over me during the visit to the ruins. Then, stepping out of the shower, I checked my face for any new facial hairs. Noting a few dark hairs that had started to appear on my upper lip, I rubbed in some bleaching cream. Wrapping my hair and body in a towel, I grabbed a tub of moisturising cream from on the shelf and made my way into the lounge.

Sam had returned from the beach full of beans and was grinning from head to toe.

"Looks like you have had a good afternoon!" I smiled as I took a seat on the settee.

"It was fun! How about your day? How did things go? Any adventures you want to share?" she replied as she poured herself a cold glass of water.

"You would have loved it, Sam. It was like being right back in time and surrounded by history. I had no idea that a pile of ruins could feel so romantic. The old castle ruins back home don't really compare. This was more real as they were once people's homes and businesses. It was as if you could see their ghosts right there in front of you, watching from the emptiness. One of the houses still had the barber's shop sign written on the wall. None of us have ever lived in a castle, so we can't put it into context. But this was almost as I imagined things to be if a pandemic wiped out the human race. In the aftermath, everything being reclaimed by nature and then stumbled upon by a few survivors many years later."

"Sounds amazing! How's our very own Zsa Zsa Gabor? What has she got planned for us tonight?"

"I have no idea. I pretty much jumped in the shower when she arrived. She was necking back the tequila then, so don't expect a quiet one," I said, taking a healthy amount of the moisturising cream and smothering it over my sensitive skin, as Julie joined us from outside.

"What on earth are you slapping all over your stubby little legs, darling? Let me see! Let me see!" she said, reaching for the tub of cream and taking it from my hand. "Don't you know what this is! This is my La Mer moisturiser you are plastering over you! At £160 a fingertip full, it's the Gucci of all skin creams, and you are lathering yourself with it as if it's a pot of Nivea from Boots! This is made from sea kelp, hand-harvested from the bottom of the Pacific Ocean during a full moon by virgins. Then mixed with donkey sperm before being shipped across the world to keep me looking gorgeous! Scrape it off, darling, and put it back in the pot! Scrape it off quickly before it sinks in and you turn into a toddler!!"

She didn't have to ask twice. The thought of covering myself with donkey sperm in a quest for eternal youth was enough to turn my stomach.

"So where are we going tonight, then Julie? I am not going out to sea if you have that planned. My legs are staying firmly on solid ground," Sam asked as she headed to her bedroom to grab a towel.

"Actually, we are going to spend an evening at a vineyard, tasting local wines and dining under the stars on a five-star meal made by a Michelin star chef! We have a limo picking us up at 7pm so don't take too long, Sammie dear, and make an effort. I need to get myself looking gorgeous too!"

Chapter 14

The drive to the vineyard had skirted the coast road north towards Argostoli. The landscape was so lush even through the middle of summer, which was not something I had expected. Greece was always portrayed as very barren and dusty in almost every programme or film I had ever seen about the country. This gave me the idea that the island potentially had a vast amount of rainfall at some point through the seasons.

We arrived at the vineyard not long after 7:30pm. The terracotta villa was vast and stood out against the deep blue sky, almost blending into the sand coloured soil beneath my feet. As we made our way through the wrought iron gates and along the limestone pathway towards the rear of the property, my senses came alive. The winery was set on a plateau above a golden sandy beach, looking out over the Ionian Sea's turquoise hues. A small islet with what appeared to be a little white church perched on top sat peacefully on the horizon.

We were escorted to a table on a raised veranda that overlooked the bay below. Leaving us with a drinks menu, the waiter disappeared to allow us time to make our selection. As we studied the list of wines available, a handsome man in his late forties approached the table and bent forward, kissing Julie on both cheeks.

"Ladies, my name is Dimitris, and I wish to welcome you to my vineyards. Before you settle and order your drinks, let me take you all on a personal tour of the Robola vines. And then we shall taste some of the best wines here on the island. Leave your bags here. They will be very safe, come, come," he said, offering his hand outwards to assist Julie from her chair.

We all followed him across the gardens and through a gate that led into the fields beyond. The harsh slopping landscape had been organised into uniformed terraces of well-tended vines. A forest of black pines lay covering the mountains above the terraces. Gentle sea breezes created a soothing sound as it rushed through the large angel-shaped vine leaves exposing tempting clusters of pale green fruits.

"Inhale the air, darlings, inhale and take a deep breath. The air alone must be 15% proof! Can't you almost taste the wine on your tongue? God! I am in grape heaven!" Julie said as she reached out for the biggest and juiciest grape, then popped it into her mouth.

"Divine! Absolutely divine! Is it just the white wines that you have here, sweetie, or is there any red? Not that I am that bothered, as red gives me a ghastly hangover and terrible wind. It is just out of interest."

"We do grow Shiraz vine for a selection of deep-bodied red wines, but Robola grapes are for white wine only. It is indigenous to this part of the Ionian islands. It has grown here for many centuries. It has been the main income source for my family for as long as I have known. I carry on the tradition from my father, his father, and so on. The Robola wine is a unique taste, a bit like citrus and peaches with a little smoke. It is very high alcohol levels too, so we drink it slowly, so we do not get too tipsy," he explained.

"Well, that's no good for you, Julie! You down a bottle quicker than anyone I know! You would be on your back quicker than usual!" Sam laughed.

"I can handle it much better than you pair of lightweights! When do we get to taste the goods, sweetie? Wandering around these vines is a little bit like foreplay. It gets a bit boring after a while!"

"Come, I will take you to the cellar where we press and store the wines after they have been harvested by hand. Then you can go back to the terrace where you will all have a taste of the selection that we sell all over the world."

Following Dimitris back towards the winery, we entered a basement. The air was cool and woody from the stacks of aged oak barrels that lay undisturbed against the far wall. A young lad wearing a t-shirt and shorts was stood barefoot in a large stainless steel vat almost filled with freshly picked grapes. He was happily squashing the wine with his bare feet as Dimitris explained that the juice from these grapes was to be collected into the barrels and then sealed to make wine.

"I hope his feet are clean and shaved sweetie! I don't want to find toes hairs in my glass!" Julie said in disgust as he happily defiled her life nectar.

It was quite a fascinating tour. I had never really considered the labour intensive process of winemaking. That little glass of relaxation was taken for granted as it was poured out of the cheap bargain bottle of booze that I would bag on a Friday afternoon in Lidl. Although I knew that there had been no handsome young Greek involved in its manufacture. Everything on the island was a lot more organic, masculine, and charming.

Dimitris led us up onto the veranda, where there was a spread of cheese, bread, and olive oil set out at our table. Several empty glasses had been lined up, ready for us to taste the final product. I stood against the railings of the veranda and momentarily looked out to sea. The breeze teased around my bare ankles, making my dress bellow out like a sail. For a moment, I felt quite majestic as the sun had started its descent into the horizon. Something inside me was disconnecting, and it wasn't my hip joint. I could really put my finger on it, but I felt different. I felt more alive than I had ever experienced throughout my entire time on this beautiful planet. I felt as if someone had flicked on a switch in my mind, and I was now wide-awake.

"Sweetie, you look like an aging Kate Winslett there in the breeze! Come sit down and get some food in you before the wine comes. Otherwise, you will be dancing naked through the vines after a few glasses!"

I took a seat and tore at a chunk of bread, dipped it in the olive oil, and took a bite as Dimitris arrived with a bottle of white Robola.

"How you like the olive oil? It is good, no? I make this from my own olives that I grow in the mountains. It is good with the Robola wine. Here please taste!" he said as he handed us all a wine glass each of deep golden liquid.

I remembered watching wine tasting once on Rick Stein's cookery programme in Italy. I tried hard to look as if I knew what I was doing and swished the liquid in a circular motion around the glass. Then I lifted the glass to my nose and took a deep snort of the sweet aroma.

"Darling, don't snort! You are not on a farm. Swill, taste, spit, and don't swallow!" said Julie as she took a sip from her glass.

"That will be a first for you, Jules!" Sam sniggered.

I couldn't help but react. It was a very quick-witted comment from Sam and made me spit the wine out all over Dimitris as I burst into laughter, then struggled to catch my breath. Tears ran down my face as I tried hard to retain my dignity.

"I am so sorry, Dimitris!" I said as I leaned forward to try to wipe off the wine-soaked crumbs of bread that had scattered out of my mouth and onto his trousers.

"It is ok! Please don't worry! I will be back in just a moment with more wine," he said, taking leave.

"Bloody hilarious Sammie, Darling! Did you know that he owns this entire estate and another two vineyards on the island? I am trying to act like the lady around him. I didn't even sleep in the same room as him last night. I don't want him thinking I am a cheap tart! I think this one could be the real deal!"

"You only met him last night, Jules! You can't know that he is right for you after just a few hours!"

"I can sweetie. I get this funny feeling when I meet someone who suits my lifestyle perfectly. And I believe that it's him. Anyway, he has invited me on his yacht for the next few days, and I don't intend to miss out on another chance of happiness. You girls will be fine without me, I am sure!"

Dimitris arrived back at the table with a red wine made from the Mavrodaphne vine. He gave us a short description of the vine's history and distinctive flavours before pouring the deep red liquid into my glass. As I took a mouthful of the ruby liquid and swilled it around my cheeks, I noted that Dimitris took a few steps back in safety.

After several glasses of wine, I was now feeling a little lightheaded again and needed a decent meal. We were joined by Dimitris and driven down to his restaurant on the beach below. As we took a seat at a table on the sun terrace, Dimitris disappeared into the kitchen, leaving us to take in the views over the bay. The sun was now giving us its final parting display. The orange afterglow had turned the sky into fire and the sea into liquid gold.

The tavern was humble and quintessentially Greek. The sweet herby aromas coming from the kitchen were mouth-watering, and I was now starving. I hadn't really eaten anything all day, and on top of all the wine we had consumed, I was beginning to feel faint. The waiter arrived with a basket of freshly baked bread and a carafe of cold water. Placing a menu on the table for us, he left as Dimitris approached the table with an elderly lady.

"This is my Mama, Fanoula. She has worked here now for almost twenty years, making people happy with her traditional Kefalonian food. The ingredients we grow in our own organic gardens are fresh and good for your bodies! The traditional Greek food keeps us looking young. My Mama, she is almost eighty and looks not much older than you beautiful ladies, no? We have a saying here where all strangers are welcomed into our homes as Philoxenia!"

Reaching her hand out, she greeted us all with a friendly smile and a Yassou! Her deep chocolate eyes were as welcoming and kind as her smile. Her grey hair was pulled back tightly into a bun away from her face. Her olive skin was soft and had little amounts of wrinkles to give away her age. It was almost as if lives were so relaxed that they had never experienced many days of stress in their lives. Other than that, the island hid a secret elixir for eternal youth hidden deep in the mountains. After giving us some meal recommendations, they both left us to look through the menu.

"I should have moved here years ago! It would have saved me a fortune on facelifts and tummy tucks!" Jules said as she looked through the menu. "I can't believe how well the Greeks age!"

"Maybe they don't frown or laugh much, which is why they have no laughter lines, unlike me!" I said as I took a sip of cold water.
"If they are laughter lines, then something in your life must have been bloody hilarious, and it wasn't your marriage to Dave! They are from all those years having

111

to think for everyone else and not putting your needs first. It's a shame that we couldn't put you in a tumble dryer just for ten minutes. Maybe you would come out wrinkle-free and three times smaller!" Julie snorted out loud.

You really had to know how to take Julie, really. Anybody listening to most of our conversations would possibly find her obnoxious and rude. Her words were sometimes a bit raw, but she was always right. I didn't take her what she said to heart. On the contrary, I found the way she looked at life refreshingly humorous. She made fun of herself just as much. She knew her flaws but made them work for her. I couldn't get to grips with mine enough to even embrace them.

Chapter 15

I was up early the next morning and feeling a little refreshed from a good night's sleep. We had left Julie at the vineyard with Dimitris and headed home in a taxi back to Spartia. After a few nightcaps in the moonlight with Sam putting the world to rights, I had retired to bed just after midnight. Being with just Sam was not quite as hectic as having Julie around. It was a little more relaxed, and I was not expected to act as if I was having a mid-life crisis.

For the next few days, we booked ourselves onto some excursions around the island. We looked beyond the familiar resorts and sought out the wild places, trying to experience as much of the culture as we could. Our adventures took us to the top of Mount Ainos, where we spotted the rare mountain violets, rugged Kefalonian ponies and hiked through citrus-scented fir trees. Sat in complete silence, we watched the world beneath us become engulfed by a dense, thick cloud only to reappear again, giving way to a vertiginous view over the entire island and surrounding seas.

We visited the capital in Argostoli to see the famous turtles, drank strong Greek coffee, and tried as many traditional sweet pastries as we could without being made to feel guilty about our weight. We sought out as many hidden coves as we could. Not one of them was the same. Some were sandy, others rockier, but the water was just as clear and enticing no matter where we ended up. We swam into coastal caves to take a respite from the hot sun, then returning to the warmth when it became cold. Chased after small shoals of fish as they darted across the pure white limestone pebbles on the seabed, searching for somewhere to hide. Floated effortlessly in the salty warm waters soaking up every essence of this Greek paradise.

During the evenings, we ate at various tavernas. I challenged my palate and ate the most incredibly delicious local cuisine. My favourites being a salted cod pie called Bakaliaropita, an octopus pie of Ktapodopita, and Chicken Tserepa. The locals were warm, welcoming, and generous, offering us fresh fruit and their stories of times gone by. The few days without Julie were blissful and much quieter.

Having a day to myself as Sam was busy catching up with emails, I had decided to take a wander down to the beach in Spartia and spend the morning lazing on the sand. I found myself a quiet corner against the rocks and settled down with another book. I don't think I had actually read so many books in my entire life as I had never actually found the time. My attention span was limited, so I always chose the cheesy romance books that always ended up with a virgin in her twenties being swept off her feet by the man of her dreams while on holiday and then sailing off into the sunset to make love under the stars.

The books were a bit of a fantasy, really, as there were no actually virgins around at that age anymore. Most had done the deed before their sixteenth birthday. It was sad, really, that romance no longer existed, I thought as I looked out at the fishing boats that bobbed up and down in the small harbour area. I felt my stomach rumble and decided to get a bite to eat. Gathering my belongings and throwing on my sarong, I wandered into the Waterway bar and waited to be seated. It was so easy to eat alone here. Nobody ever judged you as I had expected. I was much more confident in my own company. A young waitress showed me to a table on one of the terraces and took my drinks order leaving me with the menu.

"Lizzie! How are you? It has been a few days since I last saw you. I hope that you are finding your stay pleasurable." Came a voice from behind.

Turning towards the voice, I was greeted by a smiling Elias. "Yassou Elias! I have had a great time and really am enjoying myself. Would you like to join me for a drink? That is if you can. I haven't really had a chance to thank you for taking me out the other day," I said in complete shock at my own words.

"I would love to join you if that is not a problem. Please let me take your order, and I will be right back with a drink."

Giving my order of an asparagus omelette to Elias, I couldn't believe that I had been so confident and asked him to join me without any hesitation. I had never been so direct in my entire life. It was only friendly, so there was nothing else to really read into. But everything felt different, and I didn't have to hide behind the person I used to be anymore. Nobody here knew me, and I could be who the hell I wanted to be without being judged.

Elias arrived back at the table with a bottle of house wine and two glasses. He took a seat and poured us a drink, each flashing his pure white teeth at me as I melted at the gaze from his chocolate brown eyes. For a moment, I felt flustered. Not from a hot flush. This was something completely familiar. An awkward silence prevailed as I realised that I actually found this man quite attractive. I had never really looked at another man apart from Dave. But as I studied Elias, I realised that I had been going about my life blindfolded and not really considering there any other options available to me. I had pretty much written myself off from life out of fear. But what did I fear?

And then I realised that I really did not know much about this man at all. I hadn't asked him a single question about his life. I had no clue if he was married, separated, or widowed. All of a sudden, I wanted to know as much as I could about him.

"Are you married, Elias?" I said, breaking the silence as my omlette arrived at the table.

"I was married for almost twenty years but I am divorced for seven years now. My wife moved to Italy with her lover, who was my friend and worked at my bar. When I caught them in the act, it ripped out my heart and made me angry that they had betrayed me. I keep myself busy to stop me being lonely, but it is hard. How about you?" he said, taking a mouthful of wine.

"Pretty similar situation, although I was not angry. I was relieved it was over. It had become a huge dead weight that I carried around on my back, and I had no clue it was there. It is sad really as you get older you realise that you have allowed your world to become small. You grow up, fall in love, have children and forget your

116

dreams and settle for that terrible word....enough. You become accustomed to that word and sacrifice your own heart and trust it in someone else's hands. Then they end up crushing your heart. They devalue all that commitment and dedication you have given them and make you feel as it was never enough. You end up alone and realise that your life is no longer enough and you want your dreams back, but you no longer have the energy to chase them. That's why I came here, you know. Chasing the same romantic dream from these stupid books that I read, hoping to find happiness and sail off into the sunset. But now I am here, I am not sure that I want that kind of dream anymore. I am not sure what I want," I said, feeling a little sorry for myself.

"Dreams are not always found in the places we expect them to be. No matter where you run to in the world, you will never find peace if you are not happy in your heart. You are a beautiful woman, inside and out. You need to realise that you shine brighter than you know. Would you like to spend the afternoon with me on my boat?" he asked.

"Actually I would like that a lot," I smiled in response.

"Then gather your things, and we shall go now! The afternoon is perfect for a trip on the sea," he said pushing, himself up from the table and taking the bottle of wine in his hands.

Chapter 16

Elias led the way as I followed along the hot tarmac towards a small fishing boat that bobbed along on the mooring.

"Have you ever been on a boat before, Lizzie?" he asked as he jumped on board and extended his hand to help me climb onto the deck.

"Only a rowing boat on the lake in my local park, but nothing quite like this," I said as I found somewhere to sit amounts the ropes and fishing nets.

"Well, let me treat you to your first-ever time on the sea. This is the island of Odysseus so adventure is what we do best!" he announced as the engine roared to life.

Elias untied the mooring lines and gently opened the throttle. Holding onto the sides, I was thrust back just a little as I felt the boat slowly surge forward. It wasn't long before we were chugging our way along the coast. As we carved through the deep blue, I felt the gentle spray of the salty water cool my caramel skin. It only took a few seconds for the small water droplets to evaporate on my skin, leaving a circle of salt in their place. Leaning over the side, I looked into the clear blue beneath us. Even though it was deep, you could almost see straight to the bottom. Stretching my arms downwards, I cut through the liquid surface with my fingertips and felt the water tickle through my open hand.

I returned my gaze towards land. Everything looked so different from the water. There were so many hidden coves and narrow strips of white sand accessible only by boat. In places, pine-clad hills rolled sleepily downwards to be greeted by the hypnotic turquoise seas. Then as we navigated around another corner, majestic sheer white limestone cliffs rose straight out from of the sea and loomed above us. The lush green of the mountains blended into the milky blue waters in perfect harmony, making its beauty almost too much to bear.

A sudden splash next to the boat made me look again into the waters below. A dolphin had breached the surface and was playing in the wake of the boat. I squealed in delight as I shouted to Elias.

"Oh my gosh! Look, Elias! Look!" and pointed frantically at the beautiful companion that had joined us and was chattering happily as it breached the water again before diving under back into the blue. I stared at Elias, who was gently smiling back at me. I continued to watch as a few more dolphins joined in the game, and before I knew it, there was a handful to the starboard and port of the boat.

As Elias slowed the motor, they disappeared as magically as they had appeared back into the depths of the blue beneath us. I looked at our surroundings and noted that there was not a soul in sight. A long narrow strip of which sands flanked by the lush green of the rolling hills behind gave no road access from above. I could see the uniformed lines of a vineyard on the hills to the right and ruins perched on a cliff above the beach.

"I think this will be a good place for us to take a swim! This is Sissia beach, just a little south of the busier Lourdas beach. This part of the island is a little remote, and the beaches are not so easy to travel to by road. These are the places that I disappear to for some quiet," he said, stripping off his T-shirt.

His upper torso was lean and still well-toned for a man of his age. His arms wear defined and muscular. As he undid his buttons, I felt my eyes stare uncontrollably and held my breath in anticipation of what was to come before diverting my eyes just as his trousers dropped around his ankles to the floor. Why I did this, I was not sure as I had seen plenty of male bodies in my time, but none that I had desired quite as much as his. I had become so used to Dave's beer belly over the years that I have never really studied another man in so much details.

I slowly glanced back to see him stood at the edge of the boat in a skin-tight pair of speedos that on any other man would have looked hideous. But they made him even more desirable and gave me a good idea of what he had to offer. I felt the fire of my loins up react to my thoughts for the first time in a long time. In the past, whenever I got horny, all I really ever wanted was cake. Right now, there was no cake around I was craving something a little more savoury.

I pushed the thought from my mind, and as he coolly dived into the inviting waters from the side of the boat, I took a moment to quickly strip off and, as elegantly as a hippo, jumped off the edge without being seen. The water-cooled me off instantly, and the wicked thoughts that had filled my mind seconds before had quickly disappeared. It was almost like swimming in the tropics of the Caribbean. I had never experienced anything so warm and clear. It was as if I had found a part of the world where no one had yet intruded upon nature.

After a while of cooling off in the water, we climbed back into the boat and, as I rubbed myself dry, Elias poured some wine into a glass for us both. And took a seat next to me in just his speedos to allow the warm sun to dry him.

"Why is it that you not like yourself very much?" he stated as he noted me hugging the towel around my body. "Your body is perfect the way it is! It has curves in all the right places, and you should not hide it away in shame. I see many women who come to the island. They are all different shapes and sizes, yet they are never happy with the body they have. Every one of us is meant to be different. Otherwise, life would be boring!" he continued.

He was right. I shouldn't give myself such a hard time and be so ashamed of my body. Besides, nobody here knew me, and they were possibly never going to see me again, including Elias.

Reluctantly I let go of the towel and allowed it to drop around my waist.

"That is much better, no? Let the Kefalonian sunshine heal your soul!" he smiled.

"So tell me about your family here, Elias. What is it like being Greek?" I asked, taking a sip of my wine.

"So my family is kind of crazy. Greek families are very big, loud, and very protective of each other. If you dishonour one, you dishonour us all. We eat, sleep and breathe family life. There are no secrets kept in my family. It is like a bit like a telegram, telephone, tell a Greek! Before you know it, the entire village knows your business. Then, there are the Greek women. They nag, nag, nag until things get done. The men are the heads of the family, but the women are like the neck and can control the head whenever they want. Greek women are very clever at making the man think that something was his idea when really it was not. But I would not want it to be any other way. Family is what keeps you going when things go wrong," he smiled. "So is this your first time in Kefalonia?"

"It is my first time anywhere like this, actually. I have never been outside of the UK before,"

"Really? You have missed out on so many years that you have a lot to catch up on! When you go to Greece, there is no going back!"

I smiled at his answer. That thought was already flooding my mind. We sat chatting about our lives for a long while as we drank the rest of the wine and looked out over the endless sea. It was so good to be able to offload everything that I was feeling to someone who actually listened. I felt as though I could tell him anything at all.

He told me about the fascinating history of the island. The most known being the adventures of Odysseus and the Trojan War, both of which I had seen in films. Apparently the entire fleet of ships in the Trojan War had been built from the black pines that scattered the island of Kefalonia. These very firs had also been shipped to Crete and used in the construction of Knossos palace, home of the Minotaur. He told me about the ancient Achei people that had once colonised Kefalonia bringing with the mythological heroes, gods, and Mycenaean civilization. The very landscape that stood before me had been one of the very first inhabited areas of Greece. It was exactly as Sam had described, the more he told me about its history, the more I felt the island become apart of me.

Elias turned to look at me. The sun was beginning to dip on the horizon, and it was sending a warm golden glow over his face. Without thinking beyond the moment, I leaned forward and pushed my lips against his. Half expecting him to push me away in horror, I was quite surprised to feel him pull me into his arms.

Lowering me backward onto the boat deck, he gently pushed my swim costume off my shoulders and rolled them around my waist, exposing my breasts. Feeling his flesh against mine sent a surge of desire through my entire body. He began to kiss my neck, then continued working his way downwards to my large breasts before continuing towards my groin. As he removed my swimsuit from my bottom half, revealing my full womanhood and leaving me feeling very vulnerable, every part of me suddenly froze. I was completely rigid like his own personal statue of Aphrodite. I daren't look

123

down and meet his gaze as I remember that I had completely forgotten to shave!

Chapter 17

When you meet someone for the first time as you reach fifty, what they see is what they get. There is no way of them comparing you to a much younger version of yourself with flawless skin, a perfect figure, and not a stretch mark in sight. They actually like you for who you really are. This includes every wrinkle, dimple and scar you have acquired over the years. These are life's medals to prove that you survived all the shit life threw at you.

I was the one who kept comparing myself to that young girl that had once given up on her dreams and had stopped loving herself. I was the one that stared at myself in the mirror and hated what I saw because I thought I had to still look as I had all those years ago. The self-hate had manifested itself into me even more after my ex-husband had left me for someone younger. But the truth was that young girl I used to be was long gone and I really didn't want to be eighteen again. I didn't want to make myself feel shit anymore for not having a perfectly toned body or flawless skin. I had been making my own life a misery and it needed to change.

After my night of passion with Elias, everything looked and felt different. As if I had so much more to look forward to. He had made me see my body in a whole new light and given me a confidence that I had forgotten lay hidden away deep inside me. Did we sail off into the distance, fall in love and live happily ever after? Hell no! I fell in love with the island. But we did have a few more nights of passion out on his boat.

Sam and Julie left after our week's holiday, but I stayed. Partly because I could not face the return flight home and also because I was not ready to return to my miserable life back in the UK. I needed more than a week to recharge the old batteries. I rented a small villa in the ridiculously romantic and dreamy village of Assos.

While I enjoyed a large glass of ouzo on my own in one of the waterfront bars, I noted all the couples and families filling up the tables, a business idea came to mind. I set about finding the perfect place to create a small retreat specifically for middle-aged single women. The kind of women who felt a little too uncomfortable going on holiday alone, yet needed time away from their lives. Maybe after a divorce or just to learn to love themselves again as the menopausal years took the reigns for a while.

Eventually, I stumbled across the perfect place on the neighbouring island of Ithaca. With its own pool, private beach, a few acres of land for donkeys, and an ancient olive orchard, it gave all the tranquillity I was after to offer a get out of jail card to those who needed it. I am also hoping to break into the cosmetics industry to sell my own organic anti-aging face cream made from donkey milk and olive oil!

A year on, I am about to open my retreat for its very first season. Who would have known that there would be so much demand for this kind of respite? The rooms are booked out throughout the entire summer. I am also looking forward to spend some time with my best friends again as they are due to fly over this week to join me for the grand opening. Julie has been back a few times already to stay with Dimitris, with who she is head over heels in love. She has been so supportive and given me some great advice with the décor as I am not so great with that kind of thing.

Elias and I are still great friends, and he has helped me no end with the legalities of buying a place on the island. Without his knowledge and help with the language, I would never be where I am now. Both my children are proud of what I have achieved and glad that I have done something for myself for a change. I have heard that Dave is single again and living in a bedsit on his own. It makes me a little sad that he has ended up alone, but I am grateful that he cheated on me. Otherwise, I would still be stuck in Groundhog Day and would never be where I am today. I can't believe that I achieved all of this on my own.

I know that the fairy tale that we all experience at the beginning of our relationships is why we keep trying to make it through the rest of our married lives. Lasting relationships need continual work, which comes easy for some couples. But for others, they seem to shift from passionate to practical. Even though the fairy tale moments still happen in smaller fragments, married life becomes more challenging than some of us expect. No matter how far away we sail from the pettiness and demands of real life, those distant fairy tale memories anchor us in the relationship. They remind us about the myth of love we first believed in during those lust-driven years before we said our vows. Love to me isn't meant to be practical. That's why I had been happy my marriage ended. If it hadn't I would never have had the chance to love myself again and find out who I really was.

So who am I? I am Lizzie. A single menopausal, middle-aged woman in my late forties with cellulite, more wobbles than Rowntrees, and my breasts have now become more acquainted with my waistline instead of sitting quite pert on my chest where they had once spent most of their life. I am sprouting hairs in places where they shouldn't be found on a woman. My body has recently created its own tropical climate, and I am overweight for my height and age.

But guess what, I am also a strong, independent and beautiful woman who is happy and confident in her own company. I can thrive no matter what shit life throws at me. My body is just perfect and quite incredible as it wields such unique powers. It has faced the ever-changing demands my life has thrown at it. Often simultaneously being tough, tender, and fierce. It has ridden through almost forty years of hormonal storms, provided life, created food, and given a place to find comfort. It has pleased me, teased me, and tortured me along the way. It looks precisely how it is supposed to at this moment in my life. I am happy that I no longer measure my self-worth against a narrow-minded definition portrayed by the media of how women should look during each stage of their lives.

At the end of everything, we are human and not meant to be perfect. We all fall and rise, over and over. We each make mistakes that we live and learn from, allowing us to grow. We have all been hurt, but we have also survived. What a precious gift that we have been given to be alive and enjoy the simple things that make this beautiful life worthwhile. Sometimes there is sadness in our journey. But there is also lots of beauty to be experienced along the way. Even when we have been hurt and come face to face with our biggest fears, we must continue to place one foot in front of the other because if we just gave up, we would never find out what is waiting for us just around the next corner.

There is no expiry date on a dream. They do not stop because we get older. Dreams keep us believing and keep us young at heart. So no matter what your age, waist size or marital status is, if you have a dream go out there and make it happen. What else are you going to do for with the rest of your life?

Printed in Great Britain
by Amazon